GROWING UP
TALES

A Timeless Journey

GROWING UP TALES

TALES

A Timeless Journey

Sreeja Sadasivan

Clever Fox®
PUBLISHING

Chennai • Bangalore

CLEVER FOX PUBLISHING
Chennai, India

Published by CLEVER FOX PUBLISHING 2023
Copyright © Sreeja Sadasivan 2023

Illustrations by: Rahul Sadasivan
The illustrator assert the moral right to be identified as the illustrator of all images used.

To my grandparents for giving me a blissful childhood

ACKNOWLEDGEMENTS

*M*y best 'jolly' friends for always encouraging me with enthusiasm on some writeups I shared with them. My brother for pushing me to bring out this book despite many shortcomings. His illustrations, plucked right from my mind into his pencil, perfectly fit the contents. My husband always in the background, my unseen cheerleader. And my greatest and ever supportive pillar as well as discerning critic—my daughter.

CONTENTS

1

THOSE BANANA LEAVES

*S*ummer in Kerala was at its peak during April and May. The festivals of Vishu and Easter always fell during the school summer holidays.

Vibrant songs that matched the festivities played on the fat television at Siya's home. Renowned Malayalee singers Marcos and Yesudas appeared on the national Doordarshan channel to sing melodious devotional songs dressed in their purest whites. TV shows where singers performed on studio stages were popular in the late eighties and early nineties.

Siya always spent her summer holidays at her grandmother's home. Even though Granny's home didn't have a TV like her home, Siya's best days were spent there.

The five-year-old was up early and constantly fiddling with steel vessels in Granny's kitchen.

The kitchen was dimly lit, with a single window and two high air vents. The walls were always dirty with black soot. The attic was filled with all sorts of rubbish and firewood.

Siya played in the kitchen only for the big green trunk box standing next to the window. She was always fascinated whenever Granny opened it. Standing on tiptoe to see the small gunny sacks of pulses and grains and the ceramic jars of pickled baby mangoes or to get a piece of the dark brown jaggery—anything used to be a treat for Siya.

If her mother shooed her out of the kitchen—Granny never did that—Siya would roam alone outside the house, throwing stones at the mangoes on the trees and never hitting a single one. Seeing the child bored, her grandmother had an important task for Siya. This always happened the week when a festival or celebration was upcoming—be it Easter in summer or Onam in September.

Granny would instruct Siya to be in the living room and to look out the window over the vast stretch of property that belonged to their family. It was a terrain a level lower than the house—a plot of half acres that belonged to Granny and would later be inherited by Siya's mom.

This land roughly resembled a jungle to Siya's young senses. Rows of bright green plantain trees and gigantic brown coconut trees lined the panorama, bordered with tall teak trees.

Deep inside, a tiny stream cut diagonally across the entire plot, a "tribute" to the dirty stream that natives called "Kollam Thoodu." This water feature was lined with plenty of pineapple shrubs planted by Siya's grandfather.

Now, what was she supposed to "watch" from the living room?

On the far edge of the plot stood a small hut that faced the other way, bordered by a boundary fence. Granny grumbled they would sneak in to get the plantain leaves for celebrations! The tradition for Keralites to eat out of banana leaves on auspicious days is a norm even today.

And Siya, the vigilant one, needed to alert Granny.

"We have a lot of banana leaves! Why can't they cut a few, just like us?" Siya asked her.

"Well, they can, but they should ask us first. That is good manners."

Siya nodded, "OK, I will watch, Nana!"

Little did Siya know that this task was given to her to refrain her from interrupting the adults' chores and business in the house. Until she turned eight, Siya was

prompt with her task. After that, a realization made her boldly declare to Granny that she had better things to do!

Siya would climb and sit on the backrest of the long sofa, which they referred to as a *settee*, placed against the wall where the watch window was. This high-up position helped Siya with her lookout.

Siya stared out till her eyes watered. A plethora of nameless lush reeds and wild flowering plants were scattered all over the bed of weeds covering the ground. This place was a green planet standing all by itself, stretching as far as Siya's tiny eyes could see from the living room window.

Siya knew all the details of this "forest" as her Granny occasionally roamed inside, tightly holding Siya's hand. Granny's pursuit was the fallen bits and pieces of husk and bark from the coconut trees that could be used for firewood. Sometimes, they collected fallen coconuts, ripe pineapples or guavas.

These expeditions were always fascinating for Siya because she was never allowed to go in alone, nor was she permitted to peek into the old, broken, moss-covered well there, where bright green frogs croaked from the bottom. Granny's presence made Siya brave enough to look inside.

In the living room, Siya would be armed, ready with an empty tin of Britannia cookies and a steel spoon. That was to drum the war cry and alert her granny working in the kitchen at the other end of the house.

Siya's watch-keeping ended when an appetizing smell arose, announcing lunch was ready.

As Siya finished her day's duty and proceeded to the kitchen, she saw a stack of neatly cut banana leaves on the dining table.

"Let me give these to the neighbours before they start lunch." Grandfather hurried towards the hut.

Year after year, Siya kept this watch until she finally declared a truce. She, however, never got a chance to drum that cookie tin. Not once did she ever see anyone come by.

Decades progressed, Siya grew up, while the banana trees disappeared. No more leaves to share the joy!

Without a tinge of green on that piece of land, it was now converted into many small blocks of plots. Rows of concrete houses of varying sizes and colours appeared, bordered by high walls and black tarred roads.

Nothing will be as it used to be. Now, no one remains in the old house to instruct a grown-up Siya. Festivals came and went every year, bringing with them a longing to gaze into that green haven once again.

2

CHILD'S PLAY

*T*here was a time when lower kindergarten was all about play with some learning of the alphabet and numbers sandwiched in between—a time when children had the glory of not having to wear a uniform. The kindergarten premises were filled with rainbows of colours running around, their chatters filling the air.

These children did not use notebooks. Instead, they used slate boards, on which one could use either a slate pencil or a piece of chalk.

A four-year-old Sarah attended kindergarten with Ramu, Sabu, Babu and Shreya. They went to and fro from school together in the same cycle rickshaw. It was a local means of transport—a hatchback tricycle, even more popular than the Ambassadors and Fiats of the time.

They studied in the same class, and Sarah shared much with them. The candy anyone brought, pieces of crayons, the wayside sights and lots of fights!

Sarah could never keep still— in class, at home or on the rickshaw. She honked the red hooter of the rickshaw, deafening the poor rickshaw driver's ears, fidgeted about and always talked loudly to her friends.

The children played a lot in the sun, in the small school garden bordered by low, bright walls. They had a swing and a slide for extra adventure.

"Come, Sarah, we are playing on the slide now," Ramu shouted at her one day.

She started running towards him and then stopped.

"No, I don't like it." As adventurous as she was, Sarah remembered scrapping her bottom on the concrete slide. For a four-year-old, that was quite a tough decision-making! Instead, she ran to play on the building steps.

The one-story kindergarten building was quite fascinating in itself. Sarah was in awe when she discovered that her neighbouring class could be entered only by descending a few stone steps. *Her classroom wasn't like that!* She thought. The teachers' room was also lower than ground level, almost like a cellar. She loved hopping on the steps.

The main entrance with an extensive verandah opened to rooms in the centre, left and right. The old-style reddish brown tiles on the floor and the ceiling gave the place a dim, ancient ambience. But, the wide windows in each room flooded them with enough sunlight.

In reality, the building was vintage. It was the remnant of a summer house built during British times in Kerala. Whatever it was, Sarah loved her school. And her friends.

During the break, the kids had plenty of choices about where to play : the small garden, the playground or the spacious verandah in the front and the narrow one that led to the backyard of the building.

If any of the classrooms were void of their teacher, Sarah and the boys loved running up and down the classroom steps and playing 'catch'. Needless to say, Sarah was always with the boisterous Ramu, Sabu, and Babu than with the girls of her class. Some of their games ended in mild fights that usually involved one or the other getting hurt.

After school hours, Sarah's mother promptly waited at the roadside for the rickshaw to bring her back home. Sarah descended from the rickshaw by shouting "tata, tata" to her friends every single day. As she walked the little path to her home with her mother, Sarah hopped and waved to her friends till the rickshaw gradually disappeared. Mother always wondered how much energy Sarah had!

One day, after her lunch and lots of play, Sarah's mother as usual, took her for her shower. They had a typical old-style well in their backyard and no tap connection. Mother drew water from it and filled it in buckets and other large containers for household purposes.

Mother seldom took Sarah next to the well as she always jumped up and down, trying to peek in, giving her mother mini heart attacks.

Sarah waited, sitting naked on the stone step, arranging small pebbles atop each other till they fell. Mother brought a bucket full of water to the stone-tiled verandah where Sarah sat.

And then Mother saw it—a blue-black spot near Sarah's hip!

"What is this? Did you fall or hit yourself somewhere?" asked Mother. Sarah didn't reply.

"Does it hurt when I touch?" she asked again, tenderly touching the spot.

"Yes, a little," replied Sarah.

"So tell me what happened today. This wasn't there yesterday when we bathed." Mother slowly lowered her voice and asked softly.

"That is, that... that Ramu hit me and poked me with his slate," Sarah stuttered.

"Oh my! Did you two fight? Or he just took to hitting poor little Sarah?" Mother hugged her and asked.

After the shower, Mother carefully applied a balm and told Sarah not to touch the area. "*That bump on the hip isn't small. It must have been a real hard poke!*" thought mother.

The next day at school, Sarah was busy colouring an apple when she saw her mother at the door. Sarah was amazed and happy to see her in her classroom.

The class teacher went up to the door to talk to Mother.

"I believe there was a squabble, and Sarah was hit very hard. She has a bad bruise. It is not visible outside her clothes, so I wanted to inform you," Mother told the teacher earnestly.

"I am aware of the fight," The teacher looked at Mother with reproach.

"Ramuuu," the teacher called out. Mother was satisfied to know that the teacher was already aware, as she purposefully did not mention any names. Ramu stood up from his bench and came up to the teacher.

"Oh!" Mother let out a small gasp of breath as she saw him.

"So, your daughter did this to him first."

Ramu's left hand was in a cloth sling, and he held it gingerly. There was a tiny band-aid on his forehead. Mother hung her head down, then slowly raised it to see where Sarah was sitting.

Sarah was engrossed in her colouring again while Mother's face became a deep crimson. Unaware of why her mother came, Sarah was blissfully occupied with her work.

"I'm sorry, Ma'am, I apologise for Sarah. I will tell her not to get into fights again," Mother said.

"Yes, please. Sarah is the most mischievous child in this class. She just cannot keep herself out of fights and races! Always running and bumping and pushing! I wanted to talk to you, and I regret not doing so earlier! At least the boy's hand is not broken; it's only a sprain. This time!" the teacher emphasised.

Mother apologized again and left the school premises, her head still down.

That noon, as the rickshaw approached, the waiting mother was surprised to see Sarah chatting jovially to Ramu and him reciprocating with his sling-less arm around her!

Sarah said goodbye to her friends and the driver and jumped into her mother's arms. Excited, she opened her tiny palms to her mother.

"Look, Amma! Ramu gave me this!" Two glittering green marbles were enclosed in her palm.

"*Now, what am I supposed to advise this kid*?" pondered mother as Sarah skipped happily homeward.

Growing up with boys was fun!

3

UNSELECTED

*T*here was a general excitement in the grade two class. The teacher had announced an upcoming stage function at the school. The class of about 7-year-old boys and girls looked eager. The silent students all started buzzing to each other as their teacher continued that selections would soon take place for dance and drama.

"These would take place on the auditorium stage," concluded the teacher.

The students looked at each other in glee. "Wow, our show at the auditorium!"

Second graders had never been in there. They have seen older students go, but it was out of bounds for lower classes. The teacher soon demanded silence by tapping her long wooden ruler on the wooden desk. Immediately, all the students fell silent again, and the class resumed as normal.

During the break, the talk was all about the announcement they just heard. The students usually snacked at their own desks, but today, friends gathered around each other. They shared their food along with the juicy information they had now.

"It will be fun as we have never participated in such a show before," said tiny Diana.

"Oh, to just be able to be in that gorgeous school auditorium…" said a glazed Reema.

Yes, these children had not yet seen what a stage programme is. The big 3-storey building next to theirs had the auditorium on the topmost floor. They had only seen that building. These tiny tots never got a chance before to enter there.

Bhanu was excited as well, along with all her classmates. With long, lanky legs and wide feet, a size too big for her age, Bhanu towered over the others. Her thin, unhealthy-looking body frame, topped with an oily mop of hair, was always done in two long pigtail plaits. And with olive skin and protruding front teeth, Bhanu's charm lay in her ever enthusiastic spirit.

She was, however, not without friends. The students that occupied the last benches were her besties. Her height ensured that she always sat at the last bench. Vaneli, Rimi, and Sharon were all her friends—tall and hefty for their age. The bench-mates always went about together and had their snacks together.

"Mom, some kind of stage show is going to happen in school," said a bright-eyed Bhanu to her mother that evening. "I am so excited. Do they give mics to us also when we get on stage?"

"I'm not sure, dear. What did your teacher say?"

"She said tomorrow she would select the girls for the dance. There is a drama too, so they'll choose a few boys and girls."

"I hope she selects me for dance!! Can you put some cheek blush and your lipstick on me tomorrow for school?" implored Bhanu. She remembered the female cat in Tom and Jerry who always wore makeup to look pretty.

"Why, no way are you wearing makeup to school! And bless you, you don't need makeup!" chided her mother.

Bhanu went to class excitedly the next day. She saw her mother was right; nobody wore makeup or did anything spectacular. Soon, her class teacher entered and took the attendance.

"Those who want to try the dance selection try-outs, please raise your hands," the teacher said. Bhanu saw a number of hands go up along with hers.

"OK, make a line and go to the staff room. Ms Bianca is there to instruct you further."

They formed a line, with Bhanu at the tail end. None of her benchmates stood up. Vaneli beckoned Bhanu and mouthed out to return to her seat, which Bhanu ignored.

In the staff room, a tape recorder jarred Madonna's "Vogue" loudly in the background. Ms. Bianca told them, "Now face me, form a straight line and start dancing to this music." Bhanu looked at the other girls, who had instantly started shaking themselves in dance. Bhanu followed suit. She loved dancing and did a lot of frolicking at home. So, she did just the same. After a few minutes, the teacher switched off the music and asked several girls their names. To Bhanu and a few others, she asked to leave. Bhanu didn't get it that time; *was she selected?*

However, as she left the doorway, she heard the teacher say, "No bespectacled ones or rabbit teeth, so let's start practice with you, pretty girls!"

Bhanu walked back towards her classroom, the fact that she was not selected, taking time to sink in. *Did she hear right?*

When the selected girls came back, Bhanu stared at them. She thought they were cute-looking and almost the same size and height—impeccable in every way. That night,

Bhanu cried into her pillow, braving not to do so in front of her mother. Cursing her rabbit-teeth and height, she slept.

On the day of the programme, Bhanu watched as all the participating girls went to the staff room to dress up. While Bhanu and the few others lined up to watch the show, she saw the dancers giggling behind the auditorium stage.

Dressed in sunflower yellow frilly knee-high frocks with matching hair bows and transparent stockings, the girls looked like a bunch of fairies! They had a lot of shining, pink blush and lipstick on, making them look identical and pretty. The show was a huge success.

Such a success that even years after leaving school, the dance was a cherished topic of conversation when old friends chatted. Whenever someone mentioned it or shared battered old pictures, the pain bounced back for Bhanu. For her, the dance in the beautiful auditorium remained etched in her heart. The memory of the hideous remark she heard at the staff room doorway and the innocent longing of a child lingered.

Even though by then, the world hailed her as a celebrated dancer and the famous Bhanupriya danced her way to the limelight.

4

LOST

*N*oora replaced the humble lead pencil with a pen when she started class five in school. It was a moment of ecstasy for all the kids in Noora's class. All of them had bought their new gold-rimmed fountain pens filled with Chelpark ink even before the new academic year started. They gleefully switched the poor old pencils in their carry pouches.

However, Noora always had her favourites among the pencils she owned during her school days.

It was a sparkling "disco" pencil. Noora didn't know exactly why, but her classmates called it the "disco" pencil when she proudly exhibited it.

It was that shiny pencil with a sparkling and shimmering outer cover than what normal, boring lead pencils had. Some had colours that glittered like a rainbow in the sunlight, while others resembled the dancing lights you would see in a discotheque. At least, the spherical disco lights that Noora saw in movie songs had multiple flashing colours. That should be how the name came about. Noora wasn't sure if that was the actual nomenclature, but the name 'disco pencil' was popular. The pencil was indeed a beautiful diva!

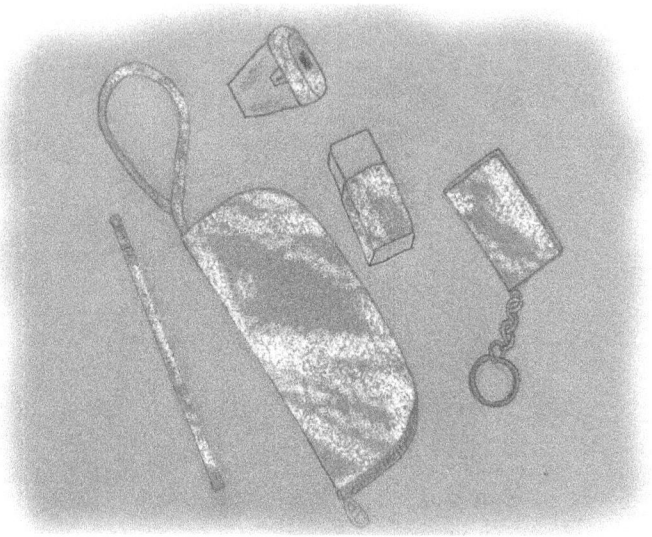

Her father had gifted her the pencils in a beautiful pencil pouch, pink in colour with glittery edges and a matching eraser and a sharpener, all befitting the status of the royal 'disco' pencil. Each had a beauty of its own and one that Noora took great pride in. The simple joys of school life!

One fine day, Noora couldn't find the entire pencil pouch in her school bag! Yes, the pouch with the two 'disco' queens and all the accessories was missing. She looked under her desk and on the floor. It was nowhere; it had simply disappeared. It became a not-so-fine day!

The pride that Noora had felt all along now melted to become one of loss and sorrow. She had a hollow feeling. She didn't know what to do. The pain of the nine-year-old was intense. She asked Anu, the girl sharing the wooden bench with her in class. But no, Anu had not seen the pouch. Instead, she suggested informing the teacher.

Reserved though she was, Noora got up from her seat and slowly went to the teacher's desk. She didn't want to miss any chance of retrieving it. The teacher asked everyone in the class to check under the desks and in their bags in case anyone had 'accidentally' taken it. The class responded by shaking their head, "No, Miss."

"Why don't you go to the other classes on this floor and ask around?" the teacher suggested.

Noora felt quite introverted but mustered the courage and went to the neighbouring classrooms.

Classes were in full swing. Noora excused herself and told the teacher present there of her predicament.

"Anyone found a pencil pouch?" the teacher asked. "What colour, child? " the teacher asked.

"Pink," Noora replied meekly, adding, "It had two disco pencils, a matching sharpener and an eraser."

"What's a disco pencil?" the teacher asked no one in particular.

All efforts were in vain; nobody had seen the treasure. Noora came back to her class, crestfallen. She couldn't pay attention to the rest of the lesson.

Noora wanted to try again. During her lunch break, she ran downstairs to the grotto. Here stood a statue of the holy Mother, enclosed in a glass case, set against a frame of grey rocks. Green shrubs and plenty of pink bougainvillaea flowers surrounded the small grotto. This grotto usually got busy during exam season when students came with prayer requests. Her friends had told her that praying to the Mother would help in such situations. Noora was hopeful. All Noora could remember was that she did lend the eraser to her fellow bench mate and couldn't recollect getting it back. But what about the pouch?

Still, she decided to double-check with Anu again. "Did you return my eraser after you borrowed it from me?"

"Of course I did," Anu was indignant.

"But I don't think so. I believe you are a stealer." Noora was so desperate.

She didn't realise that she had just then accused an innocent soul. She had thrown her first abuse at a classmate! That was the limit of her vocabulary and her patience in finding her missing stuff. Anu turned away in a huff.

The next day, during the break, Noora was once again at the grotto. Anu was there too and leaving when their eyes met. Noora didn't acknowledge her but proceeded to kneel down to pray.

Anu waited until Noora was done and said, "I also came here to pray for your pencil pouch. It was very pretty."

Days passed. By now, Noora was in acquiescence that it was gone forever. Each phase of life has varying pains. It took a long time for Noora to forget her remorse and realise that though "stealer" was nowhere in the English dictionary, she shouldn't use it on anyone!

Years ahead, during their high-school years, the guileless "stealer" girl became a friend to Noora—a friend who became so close that even years later, they laugh over the stealer episode. So close that they could effortlessly pick up any conversation left hanging from the previous year or even from a decade ago.

The pleasure of owning the glamourous pencils, then the first misery of losing them and finally gaining Anu's friendship. That was what those pencils did to Noora. She still wondered if there was indeed a "stealer" in her class or if she simply misplaced it somewhere.

She never found out.

5

ROAD TO INTELLECT

"*Y*ou must talk to that girl who always tops in class."

"But, Mum, I hardly know her. I haven't spoken to Diana ever. She sits right in the front of the class with her friends while I sit at the back," said Nithya to her mother.

Her mother glared at her.

"You both are in the same class, right? What's wrong is asking her when she woke up and how long she studied daily?"

"It's impolite to ask that!" Ten-year-old Nithya had her opinion of what was rude and what may be a peek at privacy.

She picked up her schoolbag and hurriedly left for the school bus waiting at her gate.

"If you come back without asking…." she could hear her mother's menacing voice.

Nithya loved going to school; she liked her lessons and her friends. She loved playing, too. The group of backbenchers that she sat with were her best friends.

A bright child for her age, Nithya was assiduous in her schoolwork. She loved the library and spent the class library period reading extra stuff instead of looking at the comic books that most children read.

Her friends were good company and morally good characters, though perhaps only average in academics, especially in Nithya's mother's eyes. That was the ubiquitous standard with which teachers and parents looked at children: "No good marks? Then good for nothing!"

Nithya fared third or fourth place in the class of sixty. They had a ranking system where the children were ranked according to the marks scored, based only on academics; no sports, music or extracurricular activities were taken into consideration. What you scored in English, Math, or Science determined how the teachers and most parents treated you.

Nithya's mother, though lenient in many ways, was a stickler for rank and studies. She spoke in awe of the child who got rank 1; it was always that one particular girl who bagged that. None replaced her.

Most probably, the difference between rank 1 and 2 could be a mark or two only, but no one knew that except the teacher. The distance from rank 1 to rank 2, 3 or 4 was directly proportional to the respect or taunt a child earned from her parents or teachers.

Nithya, from her backbench, could see Diana very well. She was a petite, cute girl with bright almond eyes and a head of curly hair. Nithya heartily wished that she could be Diana's friend. But Diana sat in the second row, busy in her world of friends and books. She hardly turned behind to look at the backbenchers or the 'tall' girls as they were referred.

During the break, all the students lingered on the verandah, eating their snacks or chatting with always the same circle of friends. Nithya was never brave enough to delve into any other group than her own.

A worried Nithya sat on the school bus homeward. She knew her mother would ask if she spoke to get acquainted with the 'rank 1 girl.'

Nithya's mind was disturbed as she entered the house. Her mother was smiling and served her tea and snacks. "*Maybe she forgot!*" thought Nithya; she hadn't mentioned anything so far!

After she had her fill and showered, Nithya sat down with her homework. Her mother checked her books briefly and went on to do her chores. Nithya was relieved and finished her homework in silence.

As she packed her school bag for the next day, her mother entered the room and asked the dreaded question: "So, did you speak to the bright girl?"

Oh no, not again! Nithya's face revealed that she didn't.

Her mother wore a stern look but said calmly, "All I want is for you to see how other children work hard and get good ranks in school. I want you to improve and strive for better!"

Poor Nithya bent her head, thinking about how to improve her rank from 4 to 1. That night, she lay awake pondering how to approach a girl with whom she had never conversed before.

The following day at school, the teacher shuffled the girls to play a word game. Fortunately for Nithya, she found herself sitting right behind Diana. *Well!* Nithya silently made the sign of the cross as they had taught her in her convent school.

Groups of children were teamed up during the game. Nithya soon managed to get Diana's attention and started chitchatting.

"Do you get up early and study, Diana?" asked Nithya.

Diana looked taken aback by that question, but she answered smiling, "No, I get up at 7 when my mother wakes me up."

"Oh wow, I get up at 6, and my mother asks me to do my lessons till 7," said poor Nithya. "And what do you do after school in the evening?"

"I finish my homework and study for a while, then play with my pets," said Diana. "You know I have a cat, a dog and a tortoise. I will soon get a rabbit," she said enthusiastically. "Do you have pets?"

"No," said poor Nithya. She was lost on what to ask next or even to elaborate on her boring evening routine of books and books. She had to admit that her mother did allow half an hour of television if she finished her studies.

The game was soon over, and everyone went back to their seats.

When she reached home that evening, Nithya opened up the subject herself. "Mom, Diana doesn't study in the morning. She wakes up at only 7. She does her studies for some time in the evening and then plays with her cat, dog and tortoise, " said Nithya in one breath.

Her mother looked at her. "A tortoise, indeed!"

Did she have a smile, or was Nithya imagining that?

"OK, so she seems smart to be the class topper with so little study time," said Nithya's mother, more to herself than to Nithya.

As Nithya was getting ready for bed, her mother announced, "You have to get tutored. I will speak to your class teacher to do it during lunch break."

Nithya's face was dismayed as she went to bed, staring up at the blank ceiling and lying awake for a long time.

The next day, Nithya saw her mother outside her class, talking to her class teacher, who also taught them Science.

"She is stuck to her rank 4 always! Could you do some extra coaching for her during the break? Of course, I would compensate you," coaxed Mother. Whatever was discussed, Nithya could see the teacher had agreed.

The coaching began that afternoon. Nithya had to finish her lunch as quickly as possible and then sit with her teacher in the empty classroom. She was given some notes to copy, all the while hearing the exuberant screams from her classmates playing in the playground. She was devastated. She loved running and playing in the sun during the lunch break they got. This predicament was to continue every single school day.

One day, it was Science period when the teacher asked, "So children, who brought the lemonade as discussed yesterday? Also, a straw?" Amina's hands, as usual, were already up in the air, and the teacher smiled.

"Alright, Amina, please bring them here, and we can experiment."

The science experiment was to prove that blowing carbon dioxide into lime water turns it milky white, as mentioned in the textbook. The teacher poured the lemonade into a clear glass and tried a few times to blow the straw into the juice. When nothing happened, she asked Amina to try and blow into it. Amina did it with so much force that some splattered, and lots of forth and bubbles formed, making it quite difficult to say if it turned milky or not. The class took notes.

Nithya's coaching routine continued, though she longed to shirk it. During the break every day, Nithya hurriedly ate her food and studied with the teacher.

"But mum, she isn't a good teacher. I hardly understand what she teaches, and when I check my textbooks and other books from the library, half of what she teaches seems like nonsense," said Nithya to her mother one day.

"NITHYA! How can you talk like that about your teacher?!!!" Mom looked threatening. Shutting up was the only solace for Nithya.

Yet another exam season came. Nithya studied meticulously, as she always did. She consistently managed by herself; her mother never had to sit with her or persuade her to study, though Mom checked on her occasionally.

The results were out soon. A reluctant Nithya brought the pink progress card to her mother to sign.

"Rank 5! From last term's rank 4?" Her mother looked more worried than angry.

Silently, she signed the card for Nithya. "Sorry, Mom" she timidly said. "It's OK, dear. I am sorry if I pushed you too much," came Mom's surprising reply. Nithya stared at her.

The next day onwards, the children saw that they had a new Science teacher.

Her mother said that morning, "You go and play with your friends during the break. You don't need extra coaching, and you will do well yourself."

Little did Nithya and her classmates know that Mom had complained to the school supervisor. They removed the Science teacher from class 5 and assigned her to a much lower class.

The fact that the Science teacher was experimenting with lemonade to turn it milky when "lime water" in reality meant Calcium Hydroxide* in water was a good enough reason for the management!

[** a chemical name]

6

FRIENDLY PHONE CALLS

*T*he old-age telephone was an amusing one to see. Does anyone remember how it looked like or worked in the 1990s? With a bulky body with ten digits on its face, set circular so that we use our index finger in a semicircle to dial them. The receiver sat on top, attached to its mother by a long coil of wire.

Needless to say, they permanently sat on a table. Many of our houses even had a dedicated "telephone table," which the telephone alone majestically occupied. They indeed were priced possessions of the household those days.

Which obviously meant that phones were never in our pockets like present-day mobile phones. Also, there was no way to display the caller's number unless you had a specific device called a "Caller ID" attached to the main phone. Or a caller ID phone, which was also rare and came much later to the small Kerala towns. These phones only served the purpose of calling and talking, nothing more, nothing less.

In fact, our memory capacity was way better than now; our brains knew all the familiar phone numbers memorised by heart. The numbers of neighbours, friends, relatives and all the commonly used ones remained intact in our frontal cortex.

We consulted the big fat book called a telephone directory for other calls. This was the bible of telephone numbers in the area, supplied every year by the Telecom office.

It was a day of excitement when a red telephone was first installed in Siya's home. To hear it go "*tring tring*" and when Siya's mother gave everyone a chance to pick it up and speak into the mouthpiece! It seldom rang in the early years, but by the time Siya progressed into high school, most middle-class Keralite families owned a telephone.

Siya was a full-on high schooler with all the energy and crankiness a teenager could have. The telephone was the next best friend in the evenings after school or on weekends. Most of her friends called her on that to discuss the "important" stuff, which sometimes included studies too!

One fine Saturday, her siblings and Siya were going out for the weekly household shopping with their mother. This was the only expedition they had out of the house at all. All other family outings like cinema, beaches and parks had to wait till school closed for vacations.

So, the children never missed this weekly trip. It was a chance to see the town and get a ride in the family car, with the possibility of buying 'ball' ice cream—the ones that came in small ball-like plastic containers you could play with.

As was the custom, Mother drove the car out into the road from the small front portico. Both her brothers occupied the back seat, in deep discussion about the latest cricket trump card set they wanted to buy; it was a big thing with the boys then.

Siya, being the eldest, was always given the duty to lock the house. She had to lock the front main door, then the iron grill door after that—a common feature in Kerala houses as extra protection, and finally, the front gates.

Whilst the car waited on the roadside, Siya methodically locked up all the three mentioned. One by one, she double-checked to ensure no robber could ever enter through these. God forbid a determined robber decides to climb the compound wall or knock down the thin kitchen door behind the house!

Once the task was completed, Siya proceeded to the passenger seat next to her mother's driver seat.

Then, it happened.

The telephone rang. Not once, not twice, but continuously. It was loud enough to be heard from where the car was. The grand teak telephone table stood in the living room by the open window.

Siya looked at her mother.

"Siya, go, answer it!" with a hint of anxiety, her mother urged her to check. "It may be urgent. Someone must really need to get through." The way it rang non-stop, one had to pick it up.

Siya got out of the car and unlocked the padlocked gates first. Next came the iron grill door; its lock and a padlock were undone. Then, the main wood door—two turns to free up the double lock.

The background music was of the ringing telephone. All the while, her mother watched her from the car. The bored boys proceeded into fight mode from talk mode. Siya's predicament drowned in the ringing. She ran inside and picked up the phone.

"Hello!"

"Hello! Hey, Divya, what took you so long?" Siya recognised the familiar voice. It was her best friend Mary calling to check on, goodness knows, whatever spicy topic she had for the weekend!

Siya swore at her so harshly that Mary hung up immediately after recognising the danger. Siya redid all the locking activities again, guessing Mary, by now, would have coolly proceeded to call up Divya. Siya had a bout of explaining to do to her mom.

Yes, Mary had dialled Siya's number instead of Divya's. Sometimes, dialling from memory falters! Siya forgave Mary, but forgetting was out of the question.

By the time Siya, Mary, Divya and the entire girl gang entered 11th grade, for the first time, they were given many school opportunities to regain acquaintance with the next-door boys' school.

Siya's was an all-girls school with all female teachers, female admin and ancillary staff. There was a sole male – the peon who rang the big iron school bell punctually at the designated hours to mark class periods. The girls assumed that perhaps only he could raise the heavy hammer to ring it. The females weren't hitting the gym yet in the 90s.

The class had finished a combined arts celebration day for grades 11 and 12, conducted at the girls' school. An agenda of school prayers, followed by songs, dances and band programmes performed by both schools. By the end of the day, they all got lots more friends from the other school.

Naturally, the young teens from both schools used any opportunity to cooperate with their neighbour school well. For study clarifications, notebook exchanges and any similar situations were well utilised to initiate a conversation.

Teenagers, being teenagers, indulged in harmless teasing of prospective couples and finding any excuse to talk to the neighbours. Teasing friends with someone of the opposite gender was normal and secretly enjoyed by most.

Not surprisingly, any news or discussions in either of the schools spread before the hammer hit the school bell!

One evening after school, a bored Siya decided to ring Mary. As she dialled, a plan materialised. On the third ring, Mary picked.

Taking care to "sweeten" her usually rough voice, Siya spoke, "Hey, could I talk to Mary?"

"Yes, it's me." Mary sounded cautious, trying to recollect who could be the owner of the "sweet" voice at the other end.

"Hi Mary, how are you? I'm Danny's sister. I wanted to talk to you since Danny is all praise of you here." Siya was as casual as possible.

Silence at the other end.

Siya wasn't a great mimic; she struggled to a great extent to feign her voice.

"Who? Oh, that Danny!" was all Mary said in surprise. *That Danny from the boys' school?*

In the background, Siya heard Mary's mother's voice. Ensuring to keep the conversation short, lest she got caught, Siya spoke for a few minutes. An unsuspecting Mary reciprocated happily and finally bade goodbye and hung up. Siya was sure she had a Cheshire grin even after falling asleep that night!

The last public bus stop was where the schoolchildren got off. From there, a straight road forked into a Y for the students to go to their respective girls' and boys' schools. Beyond the schools were high stone walls that overlooked the mighty Arabian Sea.

Yes, these schools were by the sea—a location not much heard of for schools elsewhere. The road from the bus stop towards the schools was a dreamy setting, flanked with rows of neat low cottages. Their compound walls were covered with green moss and low-hanging bougainvillaea trees. The bright magenta, orange and white flowers were always in full bloom amongst the fresh green leaves. The short walk on this common road gave the bus-goers a chance to talk to their peers from either school.

That morning, Mary broke apart from her girly crowd and singled out Danny, a tall lad from the boy's school.

"Hi, Danny! Your sister called me last evening!" Mary said excitedly. "I didn't even know you had my number! We spoke for a while. We are friends now!" beamed Mary.

While Danny looked dumbstruck at her, "My sister? Are you sure?"

Spectators around started noticing them now as Danny spoke quite loudly. He looked utterly confused. A few boys guffawed loudly. Some girls giggled. Dear Mary's chubby face changed instantly from white to pink to crimson. And then she left the scene swiftly, getting onto her school road quicker than the rest.

At school, Mary confronts Siya face-to-face. Siya keeps her face neutral. Until Mary saw that confused expression on Danny's face, she was flummoxed and had no clue at all. She had blindly believed the "sister's" friendly call! Then, it hit her like lightning that the voice was too familiar to go unnoticed!

"Siya, it was you, right? What all explaining I had to give my mother!!!" Mary burst out a few swear words.

She didn't talk to Siya for a few days. Not for long, though, as their friendship was as old as the big banyan tree at the bus stop! It meant a lot to make a fool of oneself in front of all those teens. The fun of those telephones!

7

PERFECT PREFECT

*T*he mid-July weather was perfect. June monsoons had subsided, leaving a coolness in the atmosphere. Rain was anticipated any day till the close of the month.

The grand pale-yellow two-story school building overlooked the Arabian Sea. On its wide-open verandah, the school principal stood with a microphone, pontificating. She presided over the morning assemblies with the teachers behind her while all the students in their navy blue uniforms neatly lined up facing her. Magenta and orange bougainvillaea flowers adorned the luxuriant trees standing in front of the building at various intervals.

The captains, also called the 'prefects' selection process, was over, and it was the big day for the swearing-in of the present captains. Five students were selected from the potential candidates to be the leaders to the two thousand students ranging from Grade 1 to 10, leaving aside the kindergarten and plus 2.

The four house flags—red, green, white and blue—and the yellow school flag were resting on the wall behind the principal. The house teachers lined up behind her, ready with the swearing-in speeches in their hands. A piece of band music for the march-past played on the music system, booming out on the grounds from the loudspeakers, only paused when speeches were made.

The five selected girls—one prefect for each house and the school captain known as the head girl—were summoned to the podium and sworn in. Each prefect was handed the respective house flag. The school flag was given to the head girl.

Many practice sessions were held a few days before this ceremony. The five girls had learned how to handle the flags and to perform the march-past in sync with the band music. So, that left little room for doubts or mishaps on the final day. For a fourteen-year-old girl, the flag on its long pole was just about the right weight, provided they had the precise balance to hold it upright.

The captains proceeded to the grounds from the assembly podium. The rest of the lined-up students, who were standing as per their classes, gradually formed four distinct rows according to their houses in height order.

A perfect formation that resembled an infantry emanated within minutes. Each prefect stood proudly afore their respective group, pompously holding the satin house flag high up.

The match-past began.

Bright sunshine, blue skies and the cadence of the waves in the background drowned in the blaring loudspeaker music. The rectangular school ground was not too big. The four groups of houses headed by their prefects, led by the head girl, would take three rounds and finish up.

Amy, the green-house prefect, happily marched, taking the lead from the house advancing before her. Her marches were perfect. With every left, right, and left, her knees rose high, and she was full of energy that rippled to her house members right behind her. Nothing was on her mind except the focus to keep marching precise and to hold the pole straight, which she did a splendid job of.

A minor commotion then happened. The 'green' group began to slow down.

Amy hesitated at first, as someone pulled at her, then gradually decelerated before finally coming to a halt, bending over to the smallest girl directly behind her.

She bent and lent her ears to the little one tugging at her, who whispered, "The flag…. Flag." She then seemed to comprehend what everyone else trailing behind her had observed minutes earlier.

The green satin flag had caught itself on one of the bougainvillaea trees behind them and happily perched there on the thorny branch. All the while, Amy, the newly sworn-in prefect, gracefully and perfectly marched forward some distance, holding only the pole!

She turned red, and beads of sweat glistened on her forehead. She silently wished for the ground to open up and swallow her up. But no, the ceremony must continue despite Amy's trepidation!

The music didn't stop. The groups marching in front had proceeded without knowing anything, while the groups behind Amy's got stuck in the traffic block.

The school peon and a few teachers rushed to Amy's side to retrieve the flag and bind it back to its parent pole. All this happened in a matter of minutes, yet to Amy, it felt like an eternity. The traffic block cleared when the flag bonded back to the pole, and poor Amy quickly regained her composure.

The ceremony was consummated as successfully as could be. The new principal, who had joined the school that year, was very proud of the grand function. This was her first major event, and Amy's, too.

In the end, the mishap demonstrated the prefect's first duty: composure under pressure in the face of unexpected challenges, even if it's an unruly flag!

School days are the best. By the time this realization comes, you will likely be parents to school-going children. The numerous delightful and amusing moments or even embarrassing ones like this, which even an adult Amy would vouch for, were some of the best school times!

8

FATHER FIGURE

*K*erala, the small coastal state in south India, boasts of many people who work abroad, especially in the Middle East. Many had flown there in the mid-70s during the oil boom. The rising oil prices created many promising jobs for Keralites that lured them there, leaving families behind.

They left behind a lifetime of happiness—their parents, siblings, wives or children—to make life easy for the same people! Sarah was one of those children. Her father worked abroad.

She talked to him regularly over letters and every weekend over the telephone. She saw him once a year when he came laden with gifts for her. The feeling of missing him never took root and that was because of someone else's presence ever since Sarah was five.

He was Chachu.

Chachu was Sarah's mother's younger sister's husband. It was a time when arranged marriages were as regular and predictable as clockwork.

Sarah saw her Chachi get dressed in a bright saree and serve tea and snacks to a strange family. The talk was that she was getting married. The prospect was the dusky, chubby guy sitting on the sofa, looking serious throughout, without a smile. Sarah's first impression of him was not great. If people didn't smile, Sarah smelled something fishy.

After the wedding, the new Chachu became a frequent visitor at her ancestral home. Sarah knew he was here to stay. Another male member was added to the family.

With time, she saw Chachu stepping up to assist. He got her the new textbooks not available in the school store. He helped get the medicines for her brother that were not there in the local medical shop. He always knew where to go for what.

The best part for Sarah was discovering that Chachu actually smiled and laughed a lot. He was always joking and teasing and positively lifting the general mood in the house! He loved singing and was an ardent collector of songbooks and audio cassettes.

She was awed; that was not at all how she had considered him at the initial meeting!

Sarah, with her mother and brother, stayed separately. She wished she didn't as she loved the warmth and security she felt at her grandparents' ancestral home. A dire nervousness always prevailed at Sarah's house, especially after dusk. Their house was usually always locked, and their mother was strict about them roaming outside to play. She constantly said, "We don't have our father here, so we have to be careful."

Not anymore. Whenever Chachu got a chance, he called at their house and ensured all was well. Those short but frequent visits were something the children looked forward to. He was not a man who showered them with gifts or unnecessary talks, but his presence and jocular ways made the children feel their insecure anxiety melt away instantly.

Sarah saw a change happening now that Chachu kept visiting. Their gates and the main door that used to remain shut were not anymore. Stepping outside the home after dusk didn't feel scary when Chachu was there! Sitting at the verandah chatting, feeling the cool night air was no longer spooky!

As Sarah grew up, she soon got the companionship of two younger cousins—Chachu's daughters. Even then, Chachu never got too busy for Sarah or her brother. He managed to keep up his regular visits and offer help whenever needed. In fact, now his visits were even more enjoyable with the two girls and their cute shenanigans.

Sarah was a movie buff. Her father always took them to the movies whenever he was there. And when he wasn't, Sarah satisfied herself by gazing at the colourful film posters stuck over the public street walls or repeatedly watching the old video cassettes her father had brought.

Her mother continually trained her to be less outspoken about extravagant needs. "Remember, we don't have our father here" was a regular slogan. Though she hated hearing it, Sarah abided.

However, there were moments when Sarah's heart would swell with joy. Chachu now took her to the movies along with his family. As she grew up, she realised that Chachu made efforts not just for the basic necessities but also for room for enjoyment!

As Sarah transitioned into adolescence, she pondered how Chachu made time for his office work, his own family and the extended family, giving the right amount of justice and dedication to each relationship. She knew he was devoted to his wife and daughters, but she was aware that he considered Sarah nonetheless.

High school started giving Sarah new nightmares to cope with. She found Math difficult, and the school teacher's help wasn't enough. Sarah tried getting help from her classmates, but their support was limited. In fact, there was so much competition in her school that no one wanted to invest their time in her! At home, Sarah struggled; she tried her mother's help, all in vain.

Soon, Sarah understood that her mother had informed Chachu of her dilemma. And there he was, ready with a solution already! He enrolled her at a private centre that gives extra coaching, where she finally settled into her high school work in peace.

Sarah's final year at school was dedicated to extra coaching and attending many centres outside of school. Chachu methodically managed the late evening drops and picks after his work. She passed her school finals with flying colours.

Sarah secured university admission, located quite a distance from home. Her mother was agitated and overwhelmed with the subject and the college her daughter sought, even to the verge of annoyance with Sarah's choice.

Sarah's saviour stepped up again. Chachu got the right train tickets and took it as his responsibility to get her there on time. The long journey left them standing most of the time amongst the crowd and luggage stacked around. After he managed to find a cramped seat for Sarah and her mother, she saw that Chachu was still without one, standing in the general compartment. She slowly dozed off, with the image of Chachu crushed between the standing mass.

Sarah's friends saw Chachu so frequently to the point that many asked with disbelief, "Is he really not your maternal uncle?"

A job and then marriage followed Sarah's life, the demands of which kept her apart from her ancestral home. Every phase was touched and influenced deeply by not only Chachu's presence but also his untiring efforts.

He told her, "No matter where you go, remember that your roots are here, in this family, and in the love that surrounds you. I do not doubt that you will brightly shine wherever life takes you."

As life got busy for Sarah, she slowly drifted away. Did Chachu ever feel overwhelmed or agitated about taking responsibility for a second family? Sarah sometimes wondered. Did she take him for granted? Did she do enough justice in being his well-wisher and being available for his needs as he approached the sunset years of his life?

Sarah didn't make any effort like Chachu. But she knew he was and will always be equal to a doting father. Sometimes, water is thicker than blood!

9

EVACUATION

"*W*hat is that smell? Like some dead animal?" Swapna wrinkled up her nose and asked her mother as she walked into the gleaming white marble kitchen. She fiddled with the coffee machine for a fresh cup, ignoring the cold one that her mother, Janaki, had placed at the breakfast table a while ago.

"Look at the time you are coming for breakfast!" Janaki exclaimed in annoyance.

Swapna was a night bird. On working days, she would stay up late to study. During holidays, she stayed up late to watch movies back to back. Since she did academically well and so far her professors had no complaints about her, her mother couldn't find any reason to stop her from sitting as late as she pleased.

Swapna, doing her third year in Science at the university, had all the freedom that her brother Sohan envied her about.

"Where's Sohan?"

"He has gone to the ground to play with his friends since schools are off. Now, will you help me peel these potatoes?" her mother asked.

"Isn't the maid coming today? Let me eat something first! But this smell, yuck!"

"I know, the smell is from outside. I can't figure out what it is," Janaki agreed.

Swapna loathed house chores and secretly wished it wasn't Christmas break. Then, she thought of her mother's excellent cooking and immediately changed her mind.

"Give it to me. I'll help till the maid comes." She took the bowl of potatoes and sat on the dining table to peel. She then dialled her friend's number on the telephone beside the table. Adjusting the receiver between her left shoulder and ears, she chatted to her for a while.

"OK, I can make it. See you then." Swapna hung up.

"What happened today? That call was quick and not the usual one hour!" her mother commented, amused and sarcastic.

"Amma, please, can I go to Sania's place? We haven't met in a while."

"You already told her you are going." Her mother raised her eyebrows. "Yes, you can go. But return before dusk."

Swapna ate a quick lunch after her late breakfast and hurried to leave. The day looked dull, as if it might rain. Light rains were common in December, but not to the extent of dark black days. Swapna lived in a small coastal town with the Arabian Sea just two miles behind her house.

In front of her house was the main road bustling with busy people, and buses plied in plenty. The shops and the houses along the roadside had a lot of colourful stars and fairy lights that would be lit up at night. Yes, it was Christmas the next day, and the air was as joyful as could be.

Just that the stink hung in the air that Swapna couldn't guess what might be causing it. It reminded her of the big garbage bin near the fish market. As Swapna's bus sped away from her road towards the main street, she noticed the stench gradually dissipating. Strange!

Hardly an hour had passed at her friend's house when her grey Nokia 3310 rang.

" Yes, Amma. What is that? Alright." Swapna had a short conversation with her mother, who had called.

"So I have to leave now. Time just flew, yeah?" Swapna told her friend. "By the way, a storm is predicted, and Mother said roads might get blocked due to excessive rains, so she asked me to hurry up. She told me to take an auto-rickshaw and not the bus."

There was a procellous wind that was gaining speed by the hour. Swapna's mother was waiting by the gate and was consoled to see her.

"All TV channels are relaying a lot of news. They are predicting a hurricane or something. Anyway, you are here now!"

After the family had their dinner, Swapna's mother retired to her room. Swapna took her favourite armchair in the living room and clicked through the TV channels. She soon settled on a movie, which Sohan also watched for some time. Shortly, he went to bed while Swapna proceeded to watch another movie.

Cable TV is such a blessing, she thought. The entire house was in darkness except for a decorative LED light in the living room and the TV screen.

Time soon was past midnight. Swapna wasn't the least sleepy. She knew she could snuggle in her plush four-poster bed and sleep in late if she wanted to.

As she shifted the channel, she heard a loud metallic bang—and police sirens.

A startled Swapna dropped the remote control. The bangs continued. It seemed to be coming from their outside gate as if someone was hitting it continuously with metal.

Terrified, Swapna momentarily stuck to her seat in the dim hall. Then, she jumped and ran to her mother's bedroom. By then, Janaki was stirring from sleep; the sounds were muffled in the wood-paneled bedroom.

"Amma, something's going on. Someone's banging our gates."

"Can't be robbers for sure; they wouldn't announce their coming." Sohan was also awake now and amused with Swapna's turmoiled face.

"Let me call Amma," Janaki dialled her mother, who stayed next door. She listened more than she spoke.

"Let's open the door, Swapna. Looks like all of us have to leave this place right now." Janaki looked confused and worried as she hung up.

They saw a small mob gathered at their house gate, amongst them a police jeep. By then, Swapna's grandparents joined them from next door.

"All of you have to evacuate your houses immediately. Get what you need and go to the camps set up by authorities or any house in the inland." The police announced through the handheld loudspeaker. "We have a Tsunami warning which says that it will hit in a few hours."

The road outside Swapna's gates was so chaotic with moving people, vehicles and the police that she wondered how she heard nothing except when they banged the gates.

"What's a tsunami?" asked Sohan.

"Listen, Janaki. Pack whatever is necessary and important. Let's go to Devi's house for now and decide everything else later," Swapna's grandmother Rukmini took charge, while grandfather Shanker nodded his head. "We will get our stuff and come here in a few minutes. Get the car out."

"Swapna, don't stand and dream. Go pack what you need—some clothes and all your academic certificates. This is important. Don't leave a thing here. Sohan, get going. We can only take what will fit in the car," said Janaki and rushed to her bedroom.

A frantic Swapna checked her cupboards and stuffed what she gathered as important into a shoulder bag.

"Amma, I need another suitcase," she called out.

"Are you coming or not? We are done!" shouted her mother as she stood ready in the hallway with Sohan clutching his GI Joe figures tightly.

The outside air was very cool, and the night was exceptionally dark with no moon. The cadence of the waves was distant.

Janaki took their small Maruti car out of the porch and took a few minutes to recompose. She had never driven at night before. The car gifted by her husband was only a conveyance for small-town trips during the day. She had never even touched the headlight switch before.

"You got this?" Shanker got into the front passenger seat to guide the way forward to his worried daughter.

"Yes, I can manage." she nodded.

Rukmini, Swapna and Sohan sat in the backseat with numerous bags on their laps that heaped up to their necks. A few boxes were loaded into the boot.

As the car slowly entered the main road, Janaki turned her head to look at their house behind. Their dream home was built last year—a white mansion that materialised from Swapna's father's hard-earned money from abroad and Janaki's toil with the builders.

Blinking back a tear, Janaki focused on her driving. There was a line of vehicles on the road and police checking at every junction. Keeping a slow pace, they exited their coastal road and proceeded to the highway that would take them inland.

Devi Mema was Janaki's cousin, Rukmini's sister's daughter. Her house was among a colony of closely placed houses, which they reached after taking a lot of twists and turns on inner lanes.

Janaki parked the car as close as possible to a moss-covered broken roadside wall. The company unloaded a few bags. They formed a single file to walk through a narrow lane bordered by hedges, straining themselves with the weight of the bags slinging on them.

A groggy Devi Mema answered the door with her teen son Anand beside her. She had no telephone in the house, so the arriving party couldn't inform ahead. Yet Devi welcomed them warmly as if visitors at 2 a.m. were normal! She and Anand proceeded to make sleeping arrangements for all.

"I couldn't understand what they said on the neighbour's TV," Devi said as she settled them in her cramped hall and the single bedroom. Shanker was given the tiny living room sofa while Rukmini slept on the single cot in the bedroom. The rest laid themselves on mats on the concrete floor, side by side, whispering into the night.

"What's a tsunami?" Sohan asked again. Swapna felt her eyes drooping and didn't hear if someone answered him. Her last thought was, "*This is how people live in small houses.*"

Swapna saw 6 a.m. the next morning after a very long time. She usually never saw the sun before 10. From the general hubbub, she knew everyone else was already up.

"It says Tamil Nadu got hit last night. That smell was from tonnes of dead fish that had swept to the beach due to unusual ocean behaviour," Shanker read the newspaper aloud. Everyone else sat on the floor and listened, drinking tea. "To think I'm alive during tsunami times!"

"Ah! You got up so early?" said Sohan. Swapna glared at him.

"The bathroom is next to the kitchen." Mema pointed to her.

Swapna soon found that she didn't need any guidance to find the kitchen or the bathroom. The square house had four small rooms—the living, bedroom, kitchen and bathroom, arranged side by side in such a way you can't miss any of them.

Over a breakfast of crispy dosas, the tsunami was the only topic.

"How will we know when we can go back... home," Janaki added after a pause.

"The newspaper will tell us. Or the radio," said Shanker curtly while Anand tried to tune in a radio frequency on a small transistor. There was no TV.

"Let's pray our houses remain safe," sighed Rukmini.

Then Swapna remembered she had her Nokia in her carry bag. It just beeped when an SMS came.

"Oh, you brought that one. Let's call Father and tell him what happened," said Janaki as she realized that they hadn't informed him anything yet.

In the afternoon, Shanker and Anand went out on Anand's bicycle. They came back announcing, "They have evacuated the entire Lighthouse Road. No tsunami yet." That was where Swapna's house was.

Whenever electricity was on, the transistor jarred in the background with the latest news.

Sohan showed Anand his GI Joe collection, who asked many questions with boyish interest. The ladies got busy chatting and working in the kitchen. Shanker reclaimed the newspaper once more.

Swapna alone had absolutely nothing to do! Did no TV mean no life? She sent a response SMS to her friend who had messaged earlier. "We are still at home, maybe because we are far away from the beach," came her reply.

Bored, Swapna put the phone aside as charging it was difficult when the power kept going off.

That Christmas day was the first that Swapna spent without watching the celebrations on TV or munching special snacks from the neighbours or roaming in the town watching the décor and eating pastries.

The family cramped in the available space when Swapna learnt about Devi Mema's and Anand's life. As a single mother, she brought up Anand, educated him and even built this house of theirs.

"I'm so proud you all came to stay at my place," Devi's eyes teared.

Calamity struck the next day 26th.

The radio jarred, *"At 07:58 local time, a major earthquake in Indonesia triggered tsunamis considered to be one of the deadliest in recorded history. The massive waves, measuring up to 30 metres, created havoc in 15 different countries, killing more than 2,00,000 people. 136 people in Kerala have been killed in this disaster, and on Indian coasts, over 10,000 people have lost their lives. The worst hit in Kollam was the Karunagapally taluk, where the tidal waves virtually washed away the seashore, leaving little trace of land. Close to 1,000 houses were razed in Ahizkel village. In and around Kollam, about 20,000 people have shifted to relief camps."*

The family sat and prayed, not knowing the plight of their houses.

"When can we go back home? Will it still be there?" Sohan's eyes were round with fear. Anand put his arms around Sohan. Nobody spoke anything.

Swapna's mobile rang a few times that day. Her father wanted to talk to each of them, repeatedly asking the same questions. Swapna's world of luxury and comfort was shattered in the last 24 hours. She silently reminisced about their home—a perfect white mansion that she was in love with. It had been the family's dream home.

Swapna looked at her present surroundings. Devi Mema's munificence defined a new strength for Swapna. That one can survive alone and still have a place in this world. That one can be happy despite not being amid luxury. That wealth didn't define who helped whom. She was seeing everything in a new light.

The next day's radio announcements told them Swapna's township could return. The danger phase has passed. A very subdued family headed back in their car. They saw their mansion looming up as they approached their gates, still intact and seemingly smiling at them. A fresh attitude of relief and gratitude dawned.

Swapna saw her mother and grandparents enter the threshold with both hands folded in prayer. She realized they all were still within the protection from Above.

10

A COUSINS
MEMORABLE

*H*er mother slowly turned the car from the main road into the dusty side lane. The path and the adjoining houses on both sides were familiar to Swara, who was fifteen, the eldest of the three children in the car. Her younger brother Raj also seemed to recognise the familiar locality, commenting on this and that. Dev, the youngest, kept looking with interest but with no remarks.

Swara's parents had left her father's ancestral home many years ago to settle in a modern house in town. They had left when Dev was just months old, and the children rarely visited here.

Every house in this village boasted of expansive stretches of land around it, with jackfruit, mango, tamarind and coconut trees in plenty, unlike in the town. Her mother drove the car into an open set of gates and parked it under a mango tree in front of the house. There wasn't anyone here; Swara had expected a crowd!

Mother hurriedly put their bags in this house, which belonged to Swara's aunt's daughter. They had packed for a day's stay. Then, they proceeded to the backyard, which had a long shack with many cows and goats. Swara and her brothers felt nervous walking amongst the goats. Some were tethered outside the shed, beside which a short pathway bordered by weeds and grass led to the next house of another aunt's.

The three children walked the narrow trail like an acrobat over a rope, careful to avoid going near the goats or stepping over the various animal droppings all over the path. They saw a crowd outside the main door as they approached the adjoining house. Hysterical feminine wails were audible.

Mother and the children entered the house through the backdoor into the kitchen. The ladies there talked in low voices while some cooked on the traditional firewood furnace.

The house was filled with fumes from incense and other stuff smouldering inside empty coconut shells. It was all hazy with the smoke and the standing and moving crowd. Swara felt suffocated. She hoped none of those wailing females of her family expected her to join them as well. Following her mother's cue, Swara gathered Raj and Dev and hurriedly left the living room into the front porch.

There also was a crowd where all the villagers gathered. Swara struggled to pass through the area. Clutching her brothers' hands tightly, they pushed through and reached the vast front yard.

That was when she thankfully spotted Rajini amongst the tall tapioca plants, beckoning at her in the late afternoon sun. Rajini smiled widely and squeezed Swara's hand. It had been long since they met. Behind her stood her sister, Radha.

"Let's go to my house. All are there."

Swara was thankful to move as far away as possible from the howling but dreaded meeting the goats again. It was at Rajini's house that they had parked the car and behind which the cattle and all their ghastly droppings were.

But Rajini, instead of going towards the cowshed, turned and brought them to the other side of her home. A spacious outdoor veranda was seen.

Two small boys and two small girls, all about 5 or 6 years of age, were sitting and playing with glittering green marbles. They were children of her various relatives. Swara was at a loss to recognise who belonged to whom.

But what truly thrilled Swara was the sight of a tall boy and his elder sister sitting on the handrail and looking immersed in a newspaper. Vimal and his older sister Kamala! They were her favourite cousins! Both had to look up from their reading as Dev rushed to them, shouting gleefully.

Vimal and Kamala were older than Swara but shared an amicable friendship. Despite the distances between their residences, they managed to meet sometimes.

The mood instantly lifted, and they started chatting happily about everything in their life since they last met. Always the meticulous and disciplined girl, Kamala ensured all the children gathered there kept their voices low, befitting the current situation.

"You guys cannot yell, okay?", she told the team on the floor. "And make sure no one steps and falls over these," she said, pointing to the marbles.

Rajini went inside and got some cold water from the refrigerator for everyone. Even though the house was a typical old-styled one, with its tiled roof and rough stone floors, it was equipped with all modern appliances.

Rajini and Swara were of the same age and in the same grade, so they started talking about school when Vimal demanded, "Can you both shut up? Let us play something."

All approved, but an argument soon arose about what they could play without attracting the elders' attention in the next house.

Before they could decide, "Hey guys!!!!" screamed Harsh and his sister Piya. These cousins had now arrived and rushed in to join the gang. Everyone was then talking to everyone, with poor Kamala trying to hush-hush everyone.

The area had six to seven houses that were all Swara's family. The number of cousins Swara had from her father's side was countless. Many of her cousins were quite old, as old as Swara's parents. Rajini and Radha were just two from the third generation that Swara could name without any mistakes.

However, generation differences were not a bother for the children at all. They were exultant that they were all united again, whatever the reason be. It was an era where letters and postcards still worked, and very few houses had telephones. Emails and instant messaging were unheard of.

The older children started a game of "dumb charades," which involved describing the name of a movie through acting and no speaking. Soon, squeals of suppressed laughter could be heard. The younger ones formed a different group, singing songs and still holding onto the marbles.

Swara soon forgot the time or why they were even there. For her, it was homecoming and a reunion with all her cousins. It seemed the same for everyone else, too. The games induced a lot of amusement. Soon, they were holding their sides and laughing in pure delight.

Many hours passed by when Rajini's mother came and served dinner to all the children. They sat in neat rows on the floor and ate a simple meal of rice and sautéed vegetables served on banana leaves.

After that, the younger ones were taken away to sleep by their respective mothers while the teens continued chatting into the night. Their restrained whispers drowned the chirping of crickets. The children sounded loud enough for one or the other of the adults to come around and reprimand them.

"Don't you know how you should behave?" By the third time, they were all asked to go and doze.

Sleeping arrangements were made in different houses. The children soon split up to accommodate themselves.

Swara had a tough time falling asleep in a strange bed. She occupied a tiny bedroom in Rajini's house and shared a single cot with her mother. That cramming together was an adventure in itself.

But more than the strangeness of the place, what kept Swara awake were the small sounds heard from the wooden ceiling above. The low roof had a heavy ceiling fan that gave more sound than air, but the scrapping of what Swara believed to be mice terrified her. Still, her not being alone was the only solace when she lulled herself to sleep listening to the fan, the mice and her mother's soft snores.

The next morning, Swara proceeded to the well at the front of the house; they had no washrooms inside. Next to the well was an open bathroom and a toilet—open at the top, roofless. Swara felt out of place using them.

Kamala was ready and about by now, but most of the others were still brushing their teeth by the well. Vimal was narrating what seemed like his last night's 'jumping bike' dream to a group of listening youngsters.

Swara looked around as she brushed her teeth. The side of the well had a huge citrus tree. She spotted a few yellow pomelos as big as beach balls. She wondered how the branches held with their weight.

The vast yard was covered with leaves from giant jackfruit trees, with lots of birds chirping on them. The bleat of the goats in the background and an occasional moo from the cows sounded.

Here, houses were not separated by compound walls, unlike those in Swara's town. Small, raised mounds of soil fenced around the yard perimeters, separating each property. Tufts of moss and grass grew on these mounds. Altogether, the greens, browns and various sounds all imparted a sweet freshness to Swara's senses.

Onto the same veranda proceeded all the children after a breakfast of idly and chutney. Their games, chitchats and squabbling continued with even more enthusiasm. No adult bothered them today. Rajini supplied them with water out of the fridge and packets of snacks.

Time flies when you enjoy it, and that was precisely what happened here. More people from the village came and proceeded to the house behind. Whenever anyone passed by, the children dropped their voices, only to resume with full vigour.

The morning proceeded to noon and noon to evening, with not one of the children aware of the ticking time. Soon, slanting orange twilight fell on the spacious veranda. Or rather, it fell on the children all huddled together. The floor wasn't even visible with all its occupants.

Rajini's and Swara's mothers came in to announce that only those children who could maintain quiet needed to go with them. Swara, Raj, Kamala, Vimal, Dev, Rajini and Harsh stopped their game and left the veranda. They took a side lane to the vast backyard of the next house.

The cremation was due; they could do the last rites now. This was the reason why they were all here.

Swara's father had gotten a call early morning the previous day about his father passing away, after which both her parents had immediately left. Later, her mother came back to pick up the children and pack a few things. Swara had not attended any funeral in her fifteen years and didn't know what to expect.

They proceeded slowly among the crowd to where their grandfather lay. He was covered in piles of yellow and white flowers. Peaceful, oblivious to the loud wails of his many daughters around him.

Swara paid her last respects. She was glad that just a fortnight ago, grandfather had spent almost a month with them at their townhouse. He was joyful and especially had fun with the youngest Dev. He was ill then but not bedridden and had spent his last days at each of his children's homes, including Swara's.

The sons performed the obsequies. Soon, smoke was rising from the backyard of the house—villages allowed this if there was enough land available.

Group by group, the crowd dispersed, with the children trying to keep to each other in the mob. They again went back to their familiar veranda, now subdued and pragmatic, as if the truth just sank in as to why they even got an opportunity to reunite. It was a painful truth, but time didn't stop ticking.

Soon, their parents gathered the children to be pulled back to their routine life. "*Should they wait for a death to see each other again?*" Reality struck - Swara was soon beckoned to normality. She saw herself in the backseat of her father's car with her brothers, waving at whoever was still outside there.

11

RIDE IN A WHITE PREMIER PADMINI

*S*iya loved her tuition sessions. Some of her close friends, Mary, Divya, Suhana, and Noora, and many high schoolers from other schools attended with her. Getting extra tuition after regular school hours was common in the educationally competent Kerala.

Siya loved the way her private tutor conducted the classes. Lalita Miss, as Siya and the others called her, was an easy-going, fun and meticulous teacher who knew just the right way to get her students' attention. This combination being too good to be true, Siya ensured she never missed any of her classes.

'Miss' was used synonymously with Ma'am or Madam and seldom meant an unmarried teacher. The 'Miss' was married to a professor who was a male version of herself—jovial and delightful.

Classes were at Ma'am's house, which was a yellow-painted old-style villa. The outdoors was green, with many shrubs and trees around the house and a Tulsi plant right in front. The most sought-after tree was a low luxuriant one that bore fruits that looked like cherries. The children called it the 'cherry' tree. After the class or between breaks, the students competed to pick the red fruits on it.

Outside, shimmering brilliantly in the sunlight, was the teacher's pristine white car, a Premier Padmini—a Fiat model rarely seen today. It found shelter beneath the leafy canopy of the trees if it wasn't parked in the garage adjacent to the house.

Siya and her friends always sat on the long wooden benches on the outside verandah, even though there was a room inside with an adjoining library. There was a certain satisfaction in sitting outside, enjoying the breeze and hearing the occasional sound of buses and auto rickshaws on the road just behind the house. It did get hot during summers, but the students stuck to their spots and seldom sat elsewhere.

Siya's only bother was the innumerable lizards lurking on the wooden doors and windows and between the planks supporting the brown terracotta tiled roof. Kerala's tropical climate came with creatures that weren't particularly appealing! Siya momentarily kept glancing upward to check nothing was overhead with any possibility of dropping!

"Is that your dog, Miss?" Mary asked one day. A jet-black Doberman played right next to the big well at the side of the house. Siya raised her head from her book. Yes, a lanky dog was playing there.

"Yes, what do you think? Isn't he cute?" winked the teacher.

"What will you feed him?" asked Mary again, knowing that the teacher and her family were pure vegetarians.

"*Is that all she's bothered about?*" thought Siya. She was dead scared of animals of all kinds, and this one looked anything but cute!

"Well, what I eat, he will eat. We got him last night, and he already relished my rice and sambhar," said Lalita Ma'am.

Mary and a few girls laughed out loud. They thought it was funny for a dog to be a vegetarian.

"Let's call him Ronnie, Miss," some boys sitting away listening to the conversation declared.

"If that's what you guys think, Ronnie, he is!" Miss looked as excited as them.

"*Will he always roam about free?*" Siya was about to ask the question when Ma'am said, "Those who don't like dogs, don't worry, he will not be allowed to this area where all the students sit."

Ma'am Lalita was not just a great teacher; she always sensed her students' thoughts. Siya thought Miss looked at her when she said that. Heaving a sigh of relief, Siya returned to her books.

As the calendar pages flipped, class tests and exams continued their relentless cycle. Students who took their studies seriously flourished under Lalita's care. With every upcoming end-of-year exam, Siya's batch mates spent more and more time with Lalita Miss, working out Math and Physics problems and referring to extra textbooks from the small library.

Tenth-grade board exams came along with the tensions and pressures they brought for students, parents and teachers. Lalita Miss alone remained cool. Her confidence in her students' abilities was evident.

After the exams, the friends met Lalita Miss to discuss the question papers.

"I know I got this right, but my steps weren't clear," declared Mary as they discussed a math problem.

"Mary, what is done is done. Since you all worked hard enough, relax now and let's wait for the results," said Lalita Miss.

"You are right, Miss. My head is all hot. I need to pour cold water over it," Suhana proclaimed.

The next instant, Mary bobbed up and down on her seat. She always did that when super enthusiastic.

"Miss, Miss, Miss. Will you take us all for an outing?" she always got excited when she got ideas and almost pushed the others next to her off the wooden bench they always sat on.

"That's a fantastic idea, Mary!" Miss smiled.

Siya now looked eager, her mind racing, *"What outing can they plan in their small town?"*

"Let's do a movie together?" Suhana suggested.

Siya loved watching movies at the theatre, but this past year was so hectic with studies that entertainment took a backseat.

"Yes, let us," said Mary. Siya looked at Miss expectantly.

Miss was all ears for them. The girls planned in loud, excited voices, laughing and thumping each other. In short, their discussion was so loud that it disturbed a sleeping Ronnie from the kitchen verandah, bringing him up to the 'tulsi' in the front. He always knew when excitement was in the air! Siya eyed him warily, but he didn't come any closer.

"Get your parents' permission, and I will take you all." Miss agreed to take them to a recently released movie showing in their town theatre. Since school had closed after the exams, they decided to go the very next day.

Siya got permission easily. She then telephoned Suhana, "What happened? Did your mother allow it?"

"Finally, she did after Dad convinced her!" Suhana said with a heave.

"Yay! I will come to your house tomorrow, and then we can walk together to Miss's place," said Siya before she hung up. Suhana's house was five minutes away from Ma'am's house.

No sooner had Siya hung up than the phone rang again.

"Why was your phone engaged?!" Mary was indignant to be kept waiting.

"Oh, I was talking to Suhana."

"So, are you coming? What about Suhana?" asked Mary.

"Yes, both of us!" Said Siya happily.

The next day was a lovely summer's day, and Siya woke up excited. She was so elated that she even attempted to help her mother in the kitchen, which wasn't her usual style at all! She chose her best skirt and top and got ready. Her mother gave her money for the show and the public bus to Madam's house.

A daintily dressed-up Siya took the bus that would take her to Suhana's house.

"You see to it that she is not up to any mischief," Suhana's mother told Siya. Siya nodded, smiled and thanked the heavens that her mother didn't say that about her to her friends! Why, they were both 15 and had just finished their board exams!

Suhana spent some more time doing her makeup while Siya impatiently hurried her, "Can we leave? The show starts in half an hour, and we have just about enough time to reach there!!" They giggled as they left the house and walked to Lalita Miss's house.

Mary, Anita and a few other girls were waiting there. Lalita Miss had already taken the white car out of her garage and parked it by the gate, dusted and ready to go. Ronnie lingered in the background with interest.

"What took you soooo long?" Mary burst out.

"It's her makeup," Siya pointed to Suhana.

"OK, girls, let's go?" Lalita Miss came out of the house dressed in an elegant sari and a small bunch of jasmine flowers on her long, neatly plaited hair.

'Yesssss, Misssss!!!" and all proceeded to the car.

"Where's Divya and Noora?" Siya asked Mary.

"They will come straight to the theatre as that's closer for them."

"*Which is good*," thought Siya as eight girls squashed into the Premier Padmini.

Two girls got into the front alongside Lalita Miss. The remaining six got behind. There was a lot of pushing and adjusting in the limited space.

"OK, let's go, no more bickering." Miss turned the ignition and set the gear, which was on the side of the thin steering wheel. Siya curiously watched Miss shifting the gear and driving smoothly. Not once did they feel any harsh brake or a sudden movement.

The seats were comfortable, and the pleasant smell of some flowers on the dashboard floated in the air.

"You better sit on my lap," Siya told Suhana midway as she struggled to keep her bottom in the cramped space.

The car resembled an over-packed goods lorry, which Siya had seen many times on the road. The ones that always had stacks of hay that looked like they would overflow any moment onto the road!

The girls managed to stay put inside, disregarding the crowd. The giggling and talking had no limits. Madam swiftly manoeuvred the car and parked in the lot allotted for the moviegoers. She then proceeded to the ticket counter, where Divya and Noora were already waiting. The girls gathered up together while Lalita Miss proceeded to take their tickets.

"It's my treat for you girls for studying so well!" she beamed at the girls.

Then, they climbed the stairs to the 'Grand' upper deck seating. The air conditioner was on, and the advertisements had already begun on the screen. It was one of the best theatres in their town.

The bunch of happy girls laughed, cried and smiled throughout the movie. They chattered excitedly in between, commenting on everything and miserably failing to keep their voices low.

Suhana especially couldn't contain her enthusiasm, with exuberant interjections every now and then. In contrast, Mary resorted to clutching and tapping Suhana's knees in her futile attempts to hush her down. It was a first-time experience for the friends together with their teacher.

When the movie finished, the girls were glum to leave the dark movie hall. At the parking lot, Divya, Noora,

Mary, Anita and a couple of others took leave, opting for a public bus to their homes.

As they reached the white Padmini, Lalita Miss, Siya, Suhana and two others stopped short. There was Ronnie patiently waiting for them beside the car!

"He pushed the trunk open and squeezed out!" a man holding a stack of lottery tickets called out to them from a distance. "Is he yours?" A few onlookers stared.

Miss and the girls couldn't believe their eyes! Did Ronnie sneak into the boot and travel with them?

"What's our plan, Miss?" Siya asked.

"He will have to come in with us, I suppose," Miss replied.

"Now, this is perfect for a movie day out!" Suhana laughed while Siya looked the picture of misery.

And so it was! The dolled-up teens struggled with Miss to get Ronnie in, aware of all the spectators' eyes on them.

Though the ride back was supposed to be comfortable with the reduced numbers, the girls chose to squeeze behind. Ronnie stole the show by sitting in the front next to Miss.

However, he was so well-behaved that a happy Siya felt her fear vanishing, giving the day a perfect end.

12

MOOD SWINGS

*S*akshi always had fun at her grandmother's house during the Onam holidays. Onam is Kerala's biggest festival, where the first four days are celebrated grandly by every Keralite—a universal festival beyond any differences of religion, caste or creed. Most institutions in Kerala had a few days off for the occasion.

Spending a whole week at her grandmother's was a thrilling anticipation year after year, ever since Sakshi could recollect. Breaking free of the mundane routine at her own home was something Sakshi always looked forward to.

Sakshi was five when she was gifted with a brother born during the Onam week. How thrilled she was! Now she had someone to play with, that too when the school was off!

But alas! The adults did not allow Sakshi to carry him or even put her baby brother on her lap. She satisfied herself by holding his pale white hands and legs and showing him her toys.

"Why is Rohan so pale? And look, no mosquito bites on his skin!" she had exclaimed. Her hands and legs, exposed outside her little frock, were covered with the treacherous sting marks from the flying menaces. The thick vegetation around Granny's house and plenty of water ponds made the place infamous for mosquitos. Yet, that never dampened Sakshi's spirits while at Granny's.

Granny always started the Onam preparations weeks earlier. Hanging from the dingy, smoke-filled kitchen roof were two long bunches of bright yellow bananas. Sakshi had seen her grandfather and Granny unload them from the auto-rickshaw; they had bought these from the market. Soon, they would become crispy round banana chips.

Next were clusters of a smaller version of the lighter yellow banana, which they harvested from the banana trees around the house. Sacks of dark brown jaggery, square tins of coconut oil and jute bags of various grocery items spread on the kitchen floor.

A stack of perfectly round coconuts with their husks removed was heaped at the corner. Sakshi waited for her grandfather to cut them open; she loved drinking its cool, refreshing water. Her grandfather had also kept ready the big white ceramic jars from the attic, ready to be filled with the savoury sweets Granny was due to make.

Sakshi loved the sights and smells that accompanied these holidays.

The kitchen filled up with the pleasant aroma of cooking oil, frying coconut or bubbling jaggery with cardamom powder, a smell Sakshi always associated with Onam. The sound of coconut being grated and the metallic scrapping of the long ladles sautéing the rice in the iron kadais. Excitement was in the air!

However, they didn't allow Sakshi inside the kitchen. She could only peep on tiptoe through the shut half doors of the kitchen. The door had four partitions. The lower two were almost always shut, to keep Sakshi and Rohan out. Rohan, now a toddler, had started walking and exploring.

"You stay out when I have the fire going," her Granny told her. "Now, where is Meenu? I want her in and you out, but she is never around to lend a hand!"

Granny was referring to Sakshi's mother's sister, a college-going young lady who seldom entered the kitchen.

Meenu 'mema' was the one who always put the traditional flower arrangement in front of the house each Onam till she got married and left the house. Little Sakshi tagged along with her when she searched for wildflowers on the shrubs and trees outside.

They didn't have a proper garden or flower pots, but flowers were always in plenty! Small yellow ones on the creepers on the fence, red, white and pink hibiscus that seemed to flourish everywhere, and purple button-like flowers that prostrated on the untrodden areas of the yard. Meenu collected the blooms on a banana leaf she would fold into a cone.

Sakshi watched from a distance as Meenu made a small circular patch on the white sandy ground with what looked like fresh green mud. It was cow dung, and when Sakshi knew that, she always stayed a few feet away!

Meenu Mema would arrange the flowers in circular patterns, sticking them to the patch. She did this each day of Onam, sometimes removing the dried flowers from the previous day and adding more concentric circles.

The other interesting activity for Sakshi was watching the swing being put up by the person they called "Mooppar," who regularly climbed the coconut palms to harvest the coconuts. Well, Sakshi always witnessed the putting up "ceremony." Did Grandfather wait for her to come to call Mooppar so that she could watch the doing? She supposed yes, and he always included her in all such exciting activities. Quite unlike the ladies, her mother and grandmother, who felt that children should stay out of "dangerous" stuff like the kitchen or a swing!

Mooppar was summoned every year to put up the swing at the beginning of the holidays. Sakshi never saw the swing taken off. It was always done after she returned to her house for the start of school. Grandfather would keep the coir rope ready, stored in the outside shed where he stacked the firewood and general junk.

Sakshi would squat on the ground and patiently watch as Mooppar put his prowess to work. He would diligently cut and trim the thick ends of a long coconut palm frond into a rectangular shape, just long enough for Sakshi to use as a seat. He would then climb the huge mango tree visible from the bedroom Sakshi and her mother used.

Steadily, Mooppar would climb and astutely choose a sturdy horizontal branch to tie the swing while grandfather supervised and gave instructions from the ground. Mooppar would then secure two ends of the rope and down came the two long pieces to which he tied the seat. Grandfather would then check the swing by trying his weight before setting Sakshi on it to swing to her heart's content.

It was a relatively small swing that a six-year-old Sakshi could handle. Still, Grandad always lent her a hand whenever he was free by pushing her from behind to keep it going.

The wind in her hair and skirt exhilarated Sakshi on the swing. With every backward lunge she took, she knew the forward motion would send her heart to her mouth while she felt the adrenaline rush. It was scary as well as exciting at the same time. The only activity children had those days when amusement parks or video gaming weren't even heard of in Kerala.

Sometimes, neighbouring children came by to play with her.

"You should share the swing with them. They don't have space at their homes to put up a swing," her grandfather always told her.

Sakshi spent a lot of time at the swing, either on it or playing around it. When it was time for food, her mother would beckon her from the bedroom window. Sakshi had no sense of time; eating regular food wasn't her favourite activity unless it was Granny's special Onam sweets.

"Don't take Rohan near the swing. He is too small for it," her mom warned Sakshi. Sakshi always abided by what she said. She thought her mother always looked tense and worked too hard, with her father always being away from home.

These Onam holidays, Rohan had just turned three. He was now always exploring places and running around. He loved the enormous amount of space available to play and the excitement in the air—something the children missed at their own home but found enticing at Granny's.

Now, Sakshi was struggling to bypass Rohan and go to the swing. He followed her everywhere! While she liked playing with him, she loved the swing even more. How could she swing once she was back home and the holidays were over? She would wait for Rohan's afternoon nap to get to the swing, but he now seldom napped and was always up and about!

As usual, Sakshi evaded Rohan and went to the swing one mid-morning. The adults and Rohan were busy inside the house. She started swinging first slowly and then gaining momentum.

"Chechi, me also," Rohan materialised before her, barely missing her outstretched legs, when Sakshi quickly put her feet down to stop herself from crashing into him.

Rohan looked imploringly at her. He didn't seem to have even a hint of his usual naughtiness or mischievousness about him.

"But you are too small, dear." Sakshi got down from the swing and bent down to level up with his eyes.

"Me also," he said again, pointing to the swing.

Sakshi looked around. Everyone was inside the house. She slowly lifted him, put him on her lap and sat on the swing. Rohan giggled. OK, so far so good. Sakshi held him around his chubby middle with one hand while holding the other on the rope. She pulled herself back to get the swing moving.

Rohan laughed again. That gave her more courage. She went further back a bit more and released her legs. They started swaying together. It felt good. Better than hugging her doll. With a firm grip on Rohan, Sakshi swung back and forth without any trouble that she anticipated.

The children were exultant. Sakshi felt her tension release and was proud of being the big sister, able to handle her baby brother! "*These adults…they never allowed me to carry him the past year!*" she thought.

The swinging together made her heart soar. The rush of air felt light and smelt of the nearby flowers. A few mango flowers showered when the branch shook.

After a while, Sakshi put Rohan down when her arms started aching. When she got up, Rohan wouldn't leave.

"Me again." He wasn't leaving yet and started trying to jump on the seat.

"We finished for today, again tomorrow," Sakshi tried to hold him back. "Come, now lunch, Amma would call us."

Rohan's big, doll-like eyes welled up. She thought he would now howl and make a noise, crying out. But he didn't. He only hung his head down, with a sad expression, just like the cartoon character they watched together at home on the VCR.

"OK, only one more time. OK? Then, inside we go." Sakshi told him. He nodded his head.

Since he was trying to climb by himself, she assumed he wanted to sit alone. She lifted him and put him on the seat. "Hold here with both your hands. Tight." She showed him to hold on to the two ropes on either side. He obliged. She then went behind him and slowly pushed the seat.

Yes! It started swaying with a gleeful Rohan. His laughter filled the air. A few pushes again, as Sakshi was careful to keep the movement slow. She kept running alongside the swing to ensure Rohan was alright up there. He now enjoyed the motions and was laughing all along. He soon forgot to grip well.

With a thud, Rohan fell to the ground.

The movement was too fast, and little Sakshi couldn't hold him in time. He cried out. A cry quieter than his previous laughs. He seemed to know he needed to quieten himself. He had fallen on all four, grazing his knees, both palms with dots of red. He couldn't stifle it anymore and cried out loud.

Sakshi's soaring heart was by now replaced with a no-beating heart! She panicked, not knowing what to do. She need not have worried, as she saw her mother speeding towards them within minutes. By then, Sakshi had picked the crying Rohan up and tried to rock him to consolation. Mother looked at Sakshi with anger in her eyes. Sakshi felt cold on that bright midday.

As Mother embraced Rohan and retreated towards the house, Sakshi trudged behind them. Mother washed Rohan's knees and hands from the water in a bucket by the well. His loud wail was now subdued to sobbing as it felt better with the splash of cold well water. She put Rohan on a chair in the dining room adjacent to the kitchen.

Both grandparents had now come out of the kitchen to console him while Mother rushed inside the kitchen and came out with a long knife.

Nonplussed, Sakshi watched her storm out of the house while Granny called out, "You control your temper. They are just kids."

Sakshi, now curious, went outside, following her mother. In her fit of anger, Mother simply cut the ropes of the swing! Just like that! The seat now lay on the ground, the ropes hanging in the air.

A string broke inside Sakshi.

She did not cry. Did she feel sad? She felt relieved more than sorrow, as she had believed Mother was going outside to cut a branch from the fence to give her a good whipping! That didn't happen. Instead, the swing was now reduced to two bits of rope!

"That is not how you discipline children!" chided Grandfather, his face and voice furious at Mother. "Children grow up falling and getting up is not new. You and your rules!" Grandfather stomped back into the kitchen.

"You shouldn't take out your tension on the children." Granny's voice was calmer than his as she spoke to Mother.

Days after, it was school time again, leaving Onam days, Granny's home and the sting far behind. The following year, Grandfather put up a swing again.

13

BANANA LEAVES AGAIN!

*G*owri gazed fascinated at the green paddy fields visible from her train window. Rectangular green and yellow patches edged with raised muddy kerbs rushed past.

The railway tracks went along the borders of the fields, giving the travellers a good view. Tethered cattle peacefully chewed weeds and grass undisturbed by the rushing train. They seemed to have gotten used to the unpleasant sound of the train wheels on metal tracks.

Soon, the train went on a bridge over a wide river. Bharathapuzha! Gowri had seen it in movies. She stood by the open train door and watched for a long time until the river and surrounding the white glistening reeds dissolved into the horizon.

Although most of the scenery was gorgeous, the unpleasant reality of her native land stood out. It exhibited itself in the form of colonies of tents and cloth-made makeshift houses that the poor lived in. These tents clustered near the edges of the railway tracks, where their inhabitants cooked and cleaned themselves outdoors. It was a sight too pathetic to watch.

The journey was long, Gowri's first long one by train. She had secured admission at a university that was several hours of travel by train from her hometown. Uncle accompanied her to help out, as her mother couldn't. She was relieved that he had agreed to come and support her with the admission procedures and her accommodation.

Interestingly, the train was almost filled with only students. Gowri assumed they would attend her own college. The general hustle and bustle told Gowri they were discussing everything except studies. The silent ones, she deduced, would be freshers like her.

"Shall we eat something?" Gowri didn't realise it was lunchtime till Uncle spoke. They undid the lunch packs that her mother had given them. Mother had packed their staple food of rice, curry, sautéed vegetables and fried fish on a banana leaf carefully wrapped. It was further well secured in a newspaper with a rubber band around it.

As Gowri unwrapped this, the aroma that filled the compartment was mouth-watering. She admired how her mother had neatly packed this rich assortment in a simple banana leaf. The leaf itself emanated a pleasant fragrance.

Gowri soon understood that eating out of this bundle was way more challenging and time-consuming. She somehow balanced it on the satchel bag on her lap and tried to eat quickly when the train stopped at a station.

Uncle was more extravagant and veteran in his eating style. He spread a newspaper and placed the package on the carriage seat between himself and the window. Then, he started the dig like a pro while Gowri watched, amused. She grew conscious when she noticed a few students around were also observing them—him precisely. But as no one approached or spoke to them, the lunch ordeal was completed without much ado.

On reaching, they completed the college admission formalities. Uncle and Gowri hunted for a suitable hostel for her. They first visited the college's own hostel. Gowri was welcomed by a group of staring seniors already residing there.

"You may visit the rooms," they said to Gowri. "But not him," they added, pointing to Uncle. They seemed to have more say than the hostel warden, thought Gowri.

Gowri went in with a few other newcomers and the warden. They did a quick round at the dormitories. Her decision was also quick. She went downstairs where Uncle was waiting and told him she didn't like the place.

"I knew it the moment you came down the stairs. Your face made it clear," he chuckled.

Gowri found herself somewhat surprised. She realized maybe not just him, but the senior girls now watching her would have understood that she had turned her nose up at the state of the rooms she had visited.

They then asked around for other accommodation facilities. Someone directed them to another much newer building further down the road. This one looked more like an inn, with a central main building and two wings with rows of rooms on either side. A restaurant, an Internet café, a public call booth and a glass-walled room occupied the entire ground floor.

Soon, they found that the owner of the building used the glass office. The owner gave a voracious lecture on the building facilities and the security he promised the college students.

"Let's go in and see?" Uncle turned to Gowri.

Gowri took her attention away from the owner. She had been watching intently at the way he peculiarly snorted his nose. Every time he spoke, the owner let out a pig-like sound when he emphasized certain words, and Gowri was sure he didn't even realise his unique talent. He rang his bell, and a middle-aged woman entered the room. She was the warden and proceeded to take them on the building tour. Uncle was allowed to visit the rooms as this management had a different outlook on visitors.

The two-storied building was neat and clean as can be. Some students had already occupied a few rooms.

"Each room will accommodate three girls, with a separate bed and study table. All rooms have a bathroom inside," the warden explained. "We also have a single dormitory if you prefer that." She opened a long hall with neat rows of bunk beds inside.

After they went through all the rooms, Gowri chose the first room she had seen as she came up the stairs. It had an occupant already. She smiled at the girl, and they exchanged names. Gowri knew she had found her room for the next 4 years and one of her roommates, Hema.

Uncle paid the registration fee and rent for a month in advance. The warden said the hostellers had to take food at the restaurant on the ground floor. "*That sounds much better than a hostel mess,*" thought Gowri.

"Why don't we go in and have something?" asked Uncle. Gowri nodded.

The noisy restaurant was bubbling with youngsters and buzzing with activities of all sorts. A radio banged in the background. Groups of boys and girls sat at their tables, talking and ordering food. The waiters hustled around, taking orders and trying to serve the aromatic curry in their large steel buckets, wedging their way smoothly between standing people to reach any customer who beckoned them.

A tall, see-through glass cabinet filled with an assortment of oil-fried snacks stood at the entrance next to the cashier. The cabinet door was already opened by some boys taking out snacks, loudly proclaiming what they had taken to the cashier.

Most of the male students wore the dhoti, the traditional dress that the men in Kerala wore. In fact, the general public, the students and the waiters all looked similarly dressed and very casual in how they carried themselves.

Gowri and Uncle found two empty places at the end of a long table, already occupied at the other end. Immediately came a dhoti-clad waiter who placed two banana leaves in front of them and took their order. Their food was served on the leaf, which both Gowri and Uncle relished. Uncle nodded at her. They both liked the place and the food.

What next? Uncle looked about and waved at another dhoti-clad boy a few meters from them.

"Would you clear away our banana leaves? Or do we dispose of them?" Uncle asked the boy.

The boy looked first at Uncle and then at Gowri.

Without any change in expression, he said, "You should put them in the waste bin next to the wash area."

"Thanks, not sure how you handle this place. So busy, eh?" said Uncle jovially to the boy, who chose to ignore.

Uncle bade goodbye to Gowri as she slowly settled into her room for the night. New place, new bed, new roommate, but Gowri slept blissfully, tired after the long journey and ordeals of the day.

The following day, Gowri and Hema got their third roommate, Naina. Naina's father had driven her there that morning as her home was fairly close. The trio quickly formed a close bond and went to college together—a custom that would be the same every day for the next four years!

At the college, everything went smoothly, with everyone settling into their class and teachers distributing timetables. The class had sixty students from various parts of Kerala, and every person's slang of the language was different. Gowri gradually connected each name with a face.

During any free moment, the buzz revolved around the looming presence of the senior students, who could invade their classroom for the infamous tradition known as freshers' ragging. Despite the assurances from the teachers and the Principal that no cruel or shaming levels of ragging would be tolerated, the freshers couldn't help but feel apprehensive whenever a senior strolled past their classroom door.

That first day soon ended. Gowri felt exultant as she left the college premises with Hema and Naina. The day was over without any intervention from the seniors!

As the three approached their hostel gate, Hema was the quickest to notice a gang of senior boys waiting at the restaurant entrance. The hostel's gate was the common entry gate for the restaurant and the other shops on the ground floor.

"Why are they staring at us?" asked Hema.

"Just don't look that way," was Naina's reply.

"You, stop there!" proclaimed one of the boys approaching them.

The three stopped in their tracks and looked at him. With a mop of oily black hair, too protruding eyes, and a body, though not too obese, cried out for some exercise, he looked the perfect picture of someone who could 'rag' the junior girls to misery.

"So, whom do you think you are? You two, leave," he said.

Gowri now understood he was talking to her. Hema and Naina were already walking ahead, turning their heads apologetically at Gowri.

"Come here, let's clear a few things for you," he asked Gowri to come to the restaurant entrance where more of his friends, a good bunch of senior boys, were waiting.

"Well!"

Gowri stared at the ground, her mind racing.

"You and your Uncle think my friend is a waiter?"

A confused Gowri raised her head. She had been counting the stones on the ground, unaware of how many stood before her or if any onlookers were watching. She wondered if her warden saw her from the glass office. "*Would she come to save me?*"

Moments trickled. Gowri felt claustrophobic as the boys formed a castle moat around her.

Gowri looked up at "frog eyes" and then at the person he was pointing to. Well, this was the same boy her Uncle encountered last evening at the restaurant! The same that Uncle assumed to be a waiter! He was now dressed in a tee shirt, well tucked in and casual pants. He looked every inch a college student now. How was her Uncle supposed to guess that the dhoti-clad, sweaty-looking thug was a student?!

"I didn't think like that," said Gowri quickly.

"Hmm, so see us here? Next time, pay some respect when you see us, OK?"

Gowri was relieved, "*That's it*?" she thought.

"OK," she replied, now enthusiastic.

"You will wish us good morning or evening whenever you see us!" he demanded.

Gowri nodded and slowly started to leave.

"Aha, not so fast," Frog Eyes said, "Do you have 100 rupees?"

"Me... I'm not sure," Gowri said, trying to hide the small hand wallet she held between her books.

"Check your bag. I can wait; no hurry at all," Frog Eyes winked at his friends with a supercilious smirk.

Gowri opened her wallet. It revealed a crisp, fresh 100 rupee note in its fold. She looked at Frog Eyes, who was now prying into her purse. She knew there was no way around it.

Repugnance evident, she parted with her currency. Gowri hoped he was asking for a loan and would return it. 100 rupee could buy a lot those days!

"OK, see you then! Remember what I said," he winked and turned to his friends to convey that the session was disassembled.

Gowri meandered towards Hema and Naina, who were waiting for her, a considerable distance from this gang.

Gowri was thoughtful as she climbed the stairs to her room. She mentally resolved never to ask anyone anything—to waiters or students! And never carry any money while studying at this place!

But no! Over the next four years, Gowri talked a lot. She came out of her shell and became friends with all, including the seniors. By final year, she had blossomed into a bold young adult, ready to face the world.

Needless to say, she never got her money back. A hundred rupees and an interrogative session were the cost for asking about a banana leaf disposal!

14

THEY REMAIN FOREVER...

Siya's grandparents played a huge part in her education and upbringing. They influenced her life more than anyone else.

Tara made amazing dishes, as did most grandmothers. The local festivals and celebrations were complete and enjoyable, with the sweet munchies Tara Nana lovingly made. That smell of the bubbling coconut oil and the snacks frying up in her kitchen! It still lingered around an adult Siya whenever Tara popped up in her mind.

As Siya grew up, Tara's cooking tips also increased, "You add a few drops of coconut oil to these lentils. It will enhance the sambhar's taste." A young Siya nodded but never ventured to attempt cooking or find out how Tara conjured up jars and jars of snacks.

Tara was always up and about. "You have to walk more. Or skip more. Pull yourself up the window rod for height! Then, you will want more food. Look at you! So thin, you should eat all kinds of food and be powerful. Otherwise, the wind will blow you off." Being healthy meant having substantial weight, according to Tara. Nevertheless, she never missed telling Siya about the importance of physical activities.

Tara always walked to places, seldom using public transport. Draped in her saree, hair held up in a tight bun, clutching her purse, she visited relatives or went shopping, all on foot, come rain or shine.

When Siya reached high school, computers were beginning to hold academic attention. Tara also updated herself. She used to scrutinise hard through the newspapers, informing Siya about the engineering colleges in Kerala and how the entrance exams are held, about every move of the universities where political influences on Kerala's engineering colleges were an open secret, and what computer courses were offered—anything that the papers revealed.

In fact, Siya had always seen Tara regularly read the newspaper. After finishing her chores, Tara would get comfortable on her bed, adjust the pillows and read the papers for hours.

Grandfather Bhaskar was a quiet man compared to the vigorous and impetuous Tara. He was Siya's regular tutor for any subject at school. He spoke and read English well. The number of essays and summaries he prepared for her was countless. Bhaskar was a voracious reader. Siya always found thick books in English and Malayalam at his table. However, none of them were storybooks.

Bhaskar did not believe in mere helping; he did any task wholly. He was the first man who made Siya realise that home chores should be everyone's and not solely a woman's job, as was the stigma.

He did his laundry right from drawing the well water and soaking the clothes to washing, drying and ironing them. He prepared his bathwater by heating the large aluminium vessel of water in the traditional firewood oven.

Bhaskar would be with Tara in the kitchen, too. The messy coconut jobs resided solely with him. Removing the brown course husk, opening and scraping the coconut and extracting the milk for various curries or payasam (a traditional dessert) was Grandpa's responsibility.

He was always out and about, either getting groceries, working in the kitchen garden or scrubbing at some part of the house. Siya often believed he had a touch of OCD when it came to cleanliness. From what she recollects, he was always washing something or cleaning floors!

Soon, Siya started preparing for engineering exams. Coaching classes were tedious. Bhaskar accompanied her to the early morning or late evening classes. He patiently waited until the class dismissed, ensuring Siya's safe return home at night. Siya lived next door and not in the grandparents' house. However, they were always around, helicoptering and mentoring as needed.

Siya got through her entrance exams well.

Tara's gift was opening a bank account for Siya, "You should learn to save before you spend!"

A new chapter unfolded for Siya when she secured university admission at a faraway college. With her parents' absence for unavoidable reasons, Tara and Bhaskar began planning the next steps. It was a long journey, and Bhaskar made the necessary preparations.

"Please remain calm. I will do the needful," said Bhaskar when Tara was already anticipating what all could go wrong on the journey.

On the long-distance train, jumped in the enthusiastic grandparents, with Siya and her numerous pieces of luggage, for a crucial expedition of life! The onward journey was uneventful except for Tara's constant vigilance: "Watch out for snatchers; don't put your hand out of the window! Don't go near the door! Don't sleep; we might miss the station to get down!"

When they reached, the station was crowded beyond their imagination. Bhaskar helped unload the luggage off the train, and the threesome walked in a single file, pushing through the crowd, searching for the exit.

"Dada, where is Nana?" Siya stopped Bhaskar and asked.

"What?" The noise of the crowd, the trains and the announcements were too much for the eighty-year-old Bhaskar.

Yes, Tara was not with them anymore! She must have gotten lost in the crowd.

After realizing the undesirable incident, Bhaskar pulled Siya and got to the side. Informing the station master was the only way out; it was a time when mobile phones weren't even heard of.

The station master asked them to wait until the train announcements were over. "Let's wait until Trivandrum mail has passed. It will get quiet after that."

"Tara Lakshmi Bhaskar, you are requested to come to the station master's room!" Five times, the loudspeaker echoed. Siya and Bhaskar waited at the bench inside the room, tired from the journey and apprehensive about what would happen if Tara didn't appear.

"Where did you two leave me and go?!" Tara materialised in front of the room, crying out.

Bhaskar spoke nothing, looking at his wife like he had expected this.

Siya ran to her, "Nowhere! We were in front of you, and suddenly, you let go of my hand."

"You remain quiet and just keep with me!" an annoyed Bhaskar took the luggage and pushed his way forward.

They had gone a day before the college opening day and checked into a small inn near the college.

By now, the subdued Tara was back to her boisterous self. But Siya also saw her worry.

"It's a new place and a strange inn. We have to be careful. Dada is old, and we ladies have to take care," Siya nodded. She chose not to laugh out loud and ask, "*Who went and lost herself at the station?*"

Luckily, the stay was uneventful. The next morning, the grandparents checked Siya into the college hostel and dropped her off at the college building. Siya later realized she was the only one in class to be escorted to the university with her grandparents! Everyone else either came alone or with their parents.

Bhaskar and Tara waved as Siya and the other students filed into their classes, as though to a kindergartener! An embarrassed Siya quickly disappeared inside, but it always brought a smile to her when she thought of it years later.

Four years later, Siya graduated. Bhaskar again accompanied her to distant places for exams related to employment. He waited with Siya as she got into serpentine queues extending unto the roads, in the scorching sun, alongside thousands of other job seekers. The rarity of encountering an eighty-four-year-old grandfather at such places prompted several candidates to offer him their seat if the venue had one.

Siya landed a remarkable first job, making both the grandparents proud. She took them sightseeing all over the "Silicon City" of India, where she worked, holding Tara's hand tightly as they toured the city.

Seeing them became a once-a-year occurrence after Siya relocated abroad. She saw noticeable changes in her grandparents' demeanour and appearance with each vacation visit. Their running around now changed to just walking around the house, to only sitting up on the verandah, then sitting with help at a chair, and finally getting completely bedridden. Due to the gap between each holiday visit, their changes were quite evident; various age-related diseases had seized them by then.

One day, that phone call came.

It was right after Siya had flown back to work after spending a vacation in her hometown.

Tara had passed away.

Siya was told it was quite peaceful, with her having some breathlessness while they tried to rush her to the hospital. Siya felt a lump in my throat. Siya had been with Tara the previous day before she travelled back, sitting at the dining table, chatting.

The next time Siya went to Kerala, she saw a bedridden Bhaskar, who seemed alone and lost. He appeared to miss his wife, though he mentioned nothing of that sort, except for his eyes looking a pale brown instead of black that conveyed a deep blankness.

Two more years went by. Siya got to see Bhaskar a few times during her holidays. He was beginning to look more like a skeleton with folds of wrinkled skin around them. He was a hundred years old by then. His indistinct mumble to Siya's daughter was always asking her about her studies and how she fared at school.

As in Tara's case, a morning call informed Siya that Bhaskar had also joined her. Siya would have met him in two weeks, but her vacation planning was a tad too late. He hadn't waited.

Siya did not attend either of the funerals. No regrets, either. The last she saw of them was when they were alive, and that would remain the ever-lasting and permanent image of them. When Siya last saw Tara, she was sitting peacefully, watching television, chatting with Siya. The last time with Bhaskar was when he sat at his bedside chair, chatting with Siya's daughter, smiling, holding her hands, content.

For Siya, they will forever live with life and laughter. She was glad that she did not get to see them lifeless.

Every time Siya returned home, she felt that maybe Dada had gone out to the market, and maybe Nana was somewhere around, taking her usual stroll in the yard. Siya could still see Tara's head popping up and down over the compound wall between their houses.

They'll be around forever.

AUTHOR'S NOTE

$\mathcal{P}$lease leave a review on Amazon, Flipkart and Goodreads. It will help me reach out to more readers who will be able to connect with these musings. My deepest thanks to everyone who took the time out for this.

I can also be reached on my blog page– https:// euphoricallysree.wordpress.com/contact/– or on social media using #euphoricallysree. I look forward to your feedback and hearing from you.

Milton Keynes UK
Ingram Content Group UK Ltd.
UKHW010733160124
436122UK00001B/12